Sylvie Writes a Romance

Sylvie Writes a Romance

Melissa Burovac

Copyright 2016 by Melissa Burovac
ISBN: 0990382028
ISBN-13: 9780990382027
LCCN: 2016909451
Wanderers Press, Koloa, Hi

Sylvie Jacobsen parked herself at an outdoor bar, ordered a Bloody Mary – "keep 'em coming" – and unpacked her computer. A change of scenery was what she needed to get a good start on writing her book after her failed attempts the previous evening. Sylvie had crumpled up sheet after sheet of paper, hiding all the scribbled-out words that were making her so angry; her kitchen had been littered with balls of notebook paper. At the beginning of the evening, she had made an effort to toss her failures into the trash can so she wouldn't see precisely how many attempts she had made. As the night progressed, she started simply dropping them onto the floor around her chair, which led to flicking them off the table in disgust. Eventually, she began aiming at specific objects in the room – at that point, the writing had stopped and Sylvie was simply occupying her time – and she took aim at the clock above the sink. The paper wad fell short and landed in the sink, where it stayed until this morning, when Sylvie contemplated grinding it in the garbage disposal as some sort of punishment for not being covered in clever words for her book.

Her new book had not been as easy to write as she originally thought. After publishing her first book with disappointingly mild success, she turned her efforts to something she thought would be shallow and easy just for the sake of earning money in hopes of supporting a more meaningful project. She read an article in a women's magazine that profiled three successful female authors who turned to churning out romance novels after they couldn't sell their original, headier work. When Sylvie read this, she immediately knew she could do it too.

Anyone can write a silly romance novel, she thought, and set her sights upon the millions that would roll in from lonely women all over the world.

The first book Sylvie published was inspired by a year of solo travel. As she chronicled her adventures, she secretly dreamed of making enough money to spend another carefree year away from work – work that seemed meaningless compared to her aspiration to be a travel writer. The money never appeared as planned, and she dreaded being trapped in an office until retirement. *What's so hard about writing a romance novel*, she wondered. *The story is almost beside the point if there's enough sex to keep the imagination happy; just like no one watches porn for the plot. This'll take a couple weeks of easy writing, maybe I'll write a few trashy novels, and then I can concentrate on more serious things.*

And so she began again, as she took the first sip of her bloody Mary.

> It was a dark and stormy night.

That's Snoopy. Sylvie remembered. *Try again.*

> Water dripped from his chiseled body as he emerged from the ocean. With his surfboard tucked under his arm, he walked up the beach to where she lay in the sun watching. He was tall and tan, and when their eyes met, they both knew the attraction was mutual. She longed to run her fingers through his long, curly hair as he reached behind to untie her bikini top.

Oh, that's awful. Too stereotypical.

> They spied each other from across the room, and it was like his eyes sent sparks of desire straight to her secret places...

No. No. No.

After a few flimsy attempts at this new writing style, three bloody Marys and two hours later, Sylvie was disheartened by her progress. She thought she'd at least write a chapter a day, full of sex and intrigue and beautiful people. But all she had to show for her efforts was a slight buzz and an enormous desire to get laid after trying to write about the sweaty details of sex for so long.

She glanced at the occupants of the metal bar tables, hoping to see someone to flirt with, and realized she was the only single person in a crowd of families and couples spending their Saturday by the ocean, eating lunch and looking like perfectly well-adjusted people.

Let's take it a little slower, she thought. *Maybe start with a list of words I should be using, then build a story around them.*

Heaving breasts
Voluptuous breasts
Manhood
Womanhood
Throbbing
Flesh
Seduce
Penis
Shaft
G-Spot
Come
Erection *(Oh ick)*

After an hour, she couldn't think of any more.

"Are these all the words I know? I can't write a romance novel with only 12 sex words," she said aloud to herself.

Sylvie clearly didn't have enough descriptive words in her vocabulary, so she began to Google erotic words. Aside from *nipple* and *erogenous*, everything else made her blush. She furtively kept tabs on her bar neighbors to make sure no one could see what she was reading, and guiltily half-closed her computer screen whenever anyone walked by.

Oh my God, I'm a prude.

The realization was not a pleasant one. Sylvie prided herself on being sexually adventurous and open to new things in bed, yet just whispering some of the words she found online made her blush a deep red and feel like she'd done something wrong.

I need to get over this. I don't know anything anyone would want to read in a romance novel.

And so she made a plan. Sylvie opened a new browser window and typed in the name of the most popular dating site she knew, *Waiting Hearts*. Meeting men online, going on dates, being seductive, and dressing provocatively – these were the things Sylvie was thinking of as she signed up, just to learn how to write a romance novel.

As she was finishing her last drink, Sylvie called her friend Colleen. "Help. I need a screen name for a dating site."

"It's about time you got back out there," Colleen said. "How about *FoxxyMama*? That's probably taken, though."

"Really, I'm serious. I don't actually want to find a guy to date, I just need some practice. I want to find some hot guy to talk dirty to me. So I can record it. You know, for research."

"Research?" Colleen laughed. "You've slept with plenty of guys. You know where all the parts go, what more do you need?"

Sylvie hadn't planned on telling any of her friends about her excursion into the dating world to help write her book. Somehow, it seemed embarrassing. Now she realized that she did need help, and Colleen, worldly and stylish, would be a good ally. Sylvie didn't even know how to properly wear makeup, or for that matter own high heels.

She spent the next 10 minutes explaining her plan to Colleen. "Come over this afternoon and help me make up a dating profile and see if we get any hits."

Sylvie paid her check and rushed home through light weekend traffic. Her house was high in the hills above town. Once she started thinking about bringing men home, she realized it was more isolated than she previously thought. "No one would hear me scream," she thought. Both good and bad.

Colleen arrived an hour later with a bottle of wine and a bottle of tequila.

"Pick one."

Sylvie and Colleen had met 10 years earlier in a yoga class; Sylvie was brand-new to the island and joined a women's workout group to make new friends. She wasn't the most coordinated, and never quite felt comfortable, yet she showed up three times each week and slowly began to form casual friendships. One Saturday morning after class, Colleen asked if Sylvie needed a mimosa as badly as she did; they sat at a bar all day getting to know each other, and quickly became the closest of friends.

Sylvie chose tequila to help her nerves; she had no idea why online dating made her so anxious – even fake online dating. She pulled a couple shot glasses from the cabinet, filled them to the brim, and sat next to her friend at the kitchen table. Her computer was already cued to the dating site, waiting for information to start the adventure.

"We need a good screen name," Sylvie started. "It has to seem real, nothing hokey, because I don't want to be embarrassed when I meet a guy expecting *FoxxyMama*. Something that fits me, but is a little more than me. It's got to be the screen name of a glamorous woman who might like things a little out of the ordinary."

"Glamorous women aren't on dating sites," Colleen said flatly.

"Seriously, if you're not going to help me, then go home. And I'm sorry I told you my secret." Sylvie was the kind of annoyed that meant she needed to either take a nap or start drinking more.

"Relax. Drink your tequila. Get a sense of humor – and quickly, because I think you'll need one for the guys you'll meet online. What about *SmokinSylvie*?"

"I don't want to use my real name because I don't want anyone I know to recognize me."

"Get over it. Your picture will show them who you are, anyway."

"Oh God, I hadn't thought about the picture! What am I gonna use?"

Colleen retrieved a duffel bag from the hallway. "I brought everything we need for a glamour shot, and I think I have a couple on my phone from the beach. The one of you sitting next to your surfboard is pretty hot. That should be all you need."

Crisis averted, they poured another shot of tequila and got back to work. They finally agreed upon *ShySylvie*, which could give her an excuse to be quiet or run away if she needed to. Next, it was on to the list of attributes the site required.

Do you want children? "Yes, I think I do."

Colleen stopped her from clicking the 'yes' box. "Do you want children, or does your inner sex researcher want children? We need to consider the guys you want to meet and make a profile that sounds like their ultimate fantasy. What type of guy are you looking for? For your book, I mean – not you."

"Hot. Definitely hot. But nice…although not too nice to talk dirty to me and teach me some new moves to write about. But no one who's going to tie me up and dismember me. Can I screen for that?"

"This isn't Craigslist, this is a dating site."

"Ok, 'maybe' on the kids. Don't smoke, don't do drugs…"

"I've seen you smoke pot plenty of times."

"But they don't need to know that."

"Maybe you'll find more fun guys if you're ok with drugs."

"Yeah, they'll have more fun while they're dismembering me. No drugs."

What describes your intent? "Casual dating, no commitment. Ok."

Income. Family. Longest relationship. Would you date a smoker? Headline.

"I need a headline."

Colleen poured more tequila. A headline needed creativity.

"Sexy, shy woman seeks man to seduce her."

"Oh my God, no!" Sylvie choked on her drink.

"But that's what you want, right? Might as well be truthful about it. Then you won't be disappointed by the nerds who call you and know less about romance-novel sex than you do."

"Fine, type it in. And you may as well fill in my description, too. You have 100 characters. Use them well."

> Sexy but shy, I'd like to meet a man to teach me more than I know, whether it's about surfing, or new places to hike, or whatever we try. But I want to be seduced, to feel the romance of a first encounter. I want a man who is experienced in life and knows how to treat a woman properly. If you don't know the ways to a woman's heart, please don't contact me.

"How's that? Kind of asking for sex, but not really."

"It's great. Let's take some pictures."

Colleen went back to her duffel bag and pulled out a flimsy, strapless black dress, high heels, and a makeup kit. "Put these on and I'll do your makeup and hair."

"Shouldn't I take a shower first?"

"Eh, don't bother. No one's gonna smell you through a picture."

Sylvie took another sip of tequila so she wouldn't say something she'd regret, and took the dress to the bedroom to try on. She was a little more muscular than the super-slim Colleen, and on the drunker side of tipsy, so after she writhed and squirmed into the super-tight black dress she had to sit down to catch her breath and think about the shoes. Sylvie's norm was flip-flops, from plain rubber pairs for the beach to fancy, sparkly pairs for nights out, and that was all she felt comfortable wearing. When she was younger she was embarrassed being taller than her boyfriends; she stood at exactly six feet tall, and as she aged and boys turned into taller men, she never got into the habit of wearing heels. She sometimes envied the shorter women she knew who practiced wearing heels from a very young age knowing they would never be too tall, and could wear them with grace and style by the time they were in their teens.

It was all Sylvie could do to remain upright in 3-inch stilettos at that point. She took a few tentative steps while holding onto the door frame, took a deep breath and pictured a fashion model on a runway in her mind. And instantly plummeted to the floor as her ankle turned sideways with her first catwalk step.

"Crawl to the couch; we'll practice when you're sober," Collen said, barely suppressing a laugh.

On hands and knees, Sylvie found the couch, pulled herself up, and struck what she thought was a seductive pose.

"Relax, you don't need to seduce me," Colleen told her as she walked across the living room. She deposited the tequila and shot glasses on the coffee table and retrieved the makeup bag from the kitchen. She knelt before Sylvie and stared at her face for a moment, then dumped the contents of the makeup bag on the cushion next to her. The eyeliner was the worst; Sylvie flinched and blinked and couldn't keep still with the pointy stick so close to her eyes. Colleen poured another shot for both of them. They clinked their glasses together and took a sip.

"Lay back, look at the ceiling, and I'll get your eyes done as fast as I can. And quit moving! I'm not going to stab you in the eye."

A few tries and several moist towelettes later, Colleen was pleased with the results. She brushed Sylvie's medium-length brown hair, which was naturally curly and always looked good without much help.

"Perk up those tits and let's take this picture. I have to go home and make dinner." Colleen was married with two children and had only gotten leave to take a couple hours away from her family on such short notice.

She arranged Sylvie in an easy-going yet alluring pose; legs crossed, back straight, one arm draped over the end of the couch and one arm across her lap.

"Chin up, chest out, tilt your head like a confused blonde."

Colleen snapped dozens of pictures with her Nikon; photography was one of her hobbies. Close-ups, wide shots showing the tasteful couch under local artwork of a tranquil ocean scene in Hanalei, a few of just her feet in the heels in case Sylvie wanted to attract someone with a foot fetish. Colleen wished she had brought open-toed shoes to show off Sylvie's bright red toenails. Always time for that later.

The women moved back to the kitchen table to upload the photos after Sylvie had kicked off the heels and could walk without fear of injury. They picked a close-up of Sylvie's face and a shot showing her full body and part of the living room. Colleen started to upload one of the high heel and ankle shots onto the dating site. "Oh my God, no! That's not who I want to attract!"

"Honey, if you want to write about men and sex you need to keep your options open. I don't know how many women write about foot fetishes but I doubt there's many, and it might be a lucrative option. At the very least, those shoes are hot and deserve a close-up."

Photos uploaded to the dating site, Colleen packed up her bag to go home to her family. "I'm leaving the dress and shoes. Practice every day in the heels for at least fifteen minutes so you don't break your ankle on a first date. Let me know if you get any hits on your profile and we'll decide who you should sleep with."

"Sleep with? I'm just dating for my research."

"Whatever. You need to be screwing someone anyway. Call me tomorrow."

Sylvie woke up on Sunday, later than usual, with a pounding headache. She lay in bed wishing she had pulled the blinds closed, wondering why she felt so bad. Kicking off the hot covers and glancing around her bedroom with squinty eyes, she noticed the black dress draped over an armchair in the corner, and black high heels laying on their sides where she had thrown them the night before. "Agh" was all she could say because her mouth was so dry. Her mind drifted to the day before – bloody Marys and tequila, taking photos and making a tarted-up dating profile with Colleen. With the sudden shock of remembrance, Sylvie fell out of bed in her effort to get to her computer to check her email. As she momentarily lay on the beige carpet, she half-thought about getting it steam-cleaned in case any of her dates wound up on the floor.

You never know.

She blushed from the thought.

Sylvie booted up her MacBook and pulled up her email. Thirty-nine messages in her inbox, 17 from the dating site. She stumbled into her small kitchen to brew a pot of coffee before exploring further. Nothing was possible to digest before coffee; the men who stayed up late to notice her profile, practicing with her heels, calling Colleen – Sylvie could barely keep her eyes open, much less deal with the consequences of what she had started the day before.

It was 8 o'clock when her mobile phone rang; it was Colleen.

"I let you sleep in; you seemed like you might need it. How many hits did you get on the site?"

"I have 17 messages. And my head is pounding. I almost wish I hadn't started this."

"Nonsense," Colleen replied. "Even if you never write your book, you still need to put yourself out there. I love you, but you shouldn't be spending all your free evenings at my house with my kids. That's a guaranteed way to stay single the rest of your life. And who knows, you might find someone you really like. Have you picked your first gentleman?"

"No, I haven't even looked yet. I can't do anything before coffee. And something to eat. I feel like I got hit by a truck. Can you meet me at the café in an hour?"

"Sorry, the kids have soccer. Call me if anything exciting happens."

Sylvie poured a splash of soy milk into her coffee and took her first sip, thinking about the day ahead and the chores that needed to be done – laundry, grocery shopping, picking a suitable date for research, and maybe a dip in the ocean to get rid of the hangover. She headed to the shower to get started.

Sylvie's first stop was at the café for a bagel with cream cheese. The smell of bacon frying and eggs poaching turned her stomach; bread was all she could manage at the moment. Sitting at a corner table, she looked around the room at the other diners. Just like the day before at the bar, the crowd was all couples or families with children. The two male waiters couldn't have been more than 25 years old. She didn't have anything against a younger man for her project; while she absently thought of making a second dating profile of an older woman looking for a younger man, she was in no frame of mind to be flirty. She ate her bagel and moved on to her next destination.

A Safeway had recently opened nearby and was a vast improvement over the local grocery stores. Sylvie wandered the aisles and picked out her week's worth of groceries. She went to the beauty aisle and perused items she had never looked at before: specialty face creams to fight the ravages of aging, lotions to wear at night for glowing skin – so many items promising that she could look better than she currently did. With her future dates in mind, Sylvie picked out an eye cream to apply before bed and a rejuvenation mask to use twice a week. She was a great-looking woman with just the beginnings of crow's feet around her eyes, but her confidence in attracting men had waned lately and she thought she could use a little cosmetic help.

The next aisle contained makeup – more products than Sylvie even knew existed – every shade of every color for every inch of face. Sylvie wore eyeliner to work, and that was the extent of her makeup knowledge. A fleeting feeling of pity for the women who relied on so much product ran through her mind, but that was exactly why she was standing in that aisle. She needed to be as attractive as possible for her research, or so she told herself. She pulled her phone from her reusable shopping bag and dialed Colleen's number. It went to voicemail, and Sylvie hung up without leaving a message. She could do this on her own, she thought.

"I'm a big girl." A woman standing nearby glanced at her sideways. Sylvie hadn't meant to say that out loud.

She picked out two new eyeliners, one black and one brown, and tossed them in her cart. She held different shades of lipstick against her mouth, imagining how glamorous they would make her look with her borrowed black dress and heels. She picked a dark red to look her age, and casually threw a bright red into her cart in case she wanted to appear slutty, not looking at it so she could pretend someone else had picked it out for her. Sylvie chose a random blush – they all looked the same to her – and a palette of eye shadow colors in one tray. Colleen would tell her which color to wear.

Makeup chosen, Sylvie headed for the registers. She walked past the magazine section, a plastic-wrapped row catching her eye, and stopped her in her tracks. *Must be 18 to Buy* was written in bold letters across the front of each magazine in the top shelf of the rack. Sylvie casually glanced up and down the aisle to see who was around; she didn't need any neighbors on her small island watching her check out the dirty magazines. Her curiosity was strong and her desire to be seductive won out over bashfulness. Plus no one was around, so she picked out copies of *Playboy* and *Penthouse*. Those were the only titles she recognized and felt comfortable taking to the cashier; they weren't too dirty. *For research*, Sylvie told herself, and placed them in the back of her cart under plastic bags of lettuce, just in case she ran into someone she knew on her way out. She began to think of reasons to justify these selections to the checkout clerk, whom she thought would immediately judge her as some sort of deviant. She grabbed a copy of Glamour as an afterthought and stacked it on top of the others, under the lettuce.

Shopping list complete, Sylvie pushed her cart into the checkout lane furthest from the exit, praying no one would get in line behind her. She was amazed at how fast her heart was thumping, like a schoolgirl caught doing something naughty. She reached out for the grocery divider to separate her selections from the old woman in front of her and slowly placed her items on the moving belt, making sure to keep the magazines hidden under the lettuce. Her cashier was a young man in his mid-20s and slightly overweight. Sylvie said hello as she approached, and began to dig through her wallet so she wouldn't have to look him in the eye.

"I brought my own bags," she told him as he finally reached for the lettuce, hoping to distract him. He weighed the lettuce, placed it on the other side of the counter, and picked up the Glamour magazine, scanned it quickly and placed it to the side so it wouldn't get wet from all the vegetables she was purchasing. Sylvie hastily threw her reusable bags on the counter and started throwing random items in, starting to blush as the cashier picked up the *Penthouse* magazine. He held the magazine for a long moment, looking at the cover model in pink lacy underwear under the prohibitive plastic wrap, scanned it, and placed it on the other side of the counter with Glamour. He looked at Sylvie for the first time since he started ringing up her groceries. She blushed a deep red and continued to put her items in the bags as he scanned the *Playboy* and placed it to the side with the others.

"Bachelorette party," she mumbled, continuing to not look at him. She swiped her debit card, punched in her PIN, threw the magazines in an empty bag, and headed for the exit as fast as she could, swerving around the slow people with her face still hot and red. Sylvie was definitely more modest than she realized, and silently hoped the men she would meet already had their own condoms; she wasn't sure if she could handle the stress of buying them herself if she couldn't even buy a magazine without feeling like she wanted to die. *Maybe they sell them on Amazon*, she thought. *I can have them mailed right to my house.*

Back home with her groceries unloaded and put away, Sylvie decided it was time to read her messages from the dating site. She now had 22 new messages, five more than when she woke up.

I don't know if I want to talk to anyone who has nothing else to do on a beautiful Sunday morning than sit at a computer. Again, she suddenly felt guilty because that was exactly what she was doing. *I'm hung over, it doesn't count*, she thought.

The first message was from *BigDaddy2015* and simply said, Your hot, let's hook up.

Delete. *Hopefully there's someone who put more effort into this. I can't sleep with a guy with such a blatant disregard for grammar*, she thought.

Next message. I'm coming to town, traveling from Portland. How about an adventure partner? Happy hour? I'm super fit and consider myself attractive.

Sylvie clicked on his bio to find more information. She found four pictures of *Goodlife_49*, and learned that he was a tall Sagittarius with a bachelor's degree and liked adventure. "Not bad, you're pretty good-looking for a 49 year old," she told his picture. "Only visiting, that's a positive in case he's weird." *Goodlife_49* was transferred to the "maybe" category.

Sylvie slowly made her way through the remaining 20 messages, deleting most of them for either incorrect punctuation, horrible sexist comments, long distance with no plans on visiting, pictures with ex-girlfriends not cropped out, or just unattractive. She knew Colleen wouldn't have been so picky for her, at least not with the guys who couldn't pull off correct punctuation but still looked good, so Sylvie saved those messages to look at later in case her four possibles didn't work out. She picked *Surfer1968* as her first reply; he didn't appear as anything more than a casual fling kind of guy, certainly not glamorous, but maybe she could arrange an encounter on one of the island's secret beaches if she liked him in person.

It was 4 o'clock by the time Sylvie read all her messages; she had been steadily drinking water and nibbling on chips and guacamole, and felt pretty decent after her morning hangover. She thought she needed a real drink to work up the courage to respond to *Surfer1968* and poured herself a shot of tequila from the mostly empty bottle Colleen had left behind. She sipped it slowly and began to compose her message.

> Aloha Surfer1968. I'd love to meet you for coffee or a drink. This is my first time trying online dating so I'm a bit nervous, but you look like a nice guy, and you love to surf – I do too. Why don't we meet for sunset at Salt Pond one night this week? Sylvie.

Maybe it wasn't the man Colleen would have picked, or the message she would have sent, but Sylvie was pleased with her first foray into the online dating scene. She envisioned a bronzed god rising from the ocean like Poseidon, a six-pack of abs gleaming from sweat and salt water, surfboard held under his muscular arm as he strode up the beach to where she lay on her towel, quivering with anticipation.

Get a grip, she said to herself. *He's a 47-year-old surfer with a bald spot. Not bad looking, but not much in the way of abs, either; I can give him some for my story. He has a good job and nice tan. He's my practice run, not a Greek god.*

After a dinner of salmon, quinoa and broccoli that evening, wanting to eat right to look good for her date, Sylvie put on Colleen's high heels with her grungy, green surf shorts and faded black t-shirt. She wobbled to the bathroom to explore the new purchases from the morning. She squirted the rejuvenation mask onto the palm of her hand. *Ugh, it smells like seaweed.* She applied the green goo generously on her face, according to directions, and stared at herself in the mirror. She saw a 43-year-old woman with nice, wavy brown hair, a green face, and sloppy clothes. Still staring, Sylvie peeled off her t-shirt and surf shorts.

Now she saw a woman who hadn't been running or to CrossFit in three weeks, with a green face and fading bikini lines. She set the timer on her phone for 15 minutes.

In her black cotton bra and red polka dot underwear, Sylvie carefully walked in the 3-inch heels to the living room, pushed the coffee table up against the couch, and lay on her back on the carpet, the same beige color as her bedroom. Lifting her legs off the floor, she did 25 sit-ups before her stomach started to burn and she had to rest her entire body on the floor. She could only do 16 in the next set, after a few minutes rest. As she rolled to her side to get up, Sylvie noticed the magazines she had tossed on the coffee table from her embarrassing morning shopping trip, still in the plastic wrap. She grabbed the *Penthouse*, throwing the ripped plastic on the floor next to her, and lay back down on the carpet.

Sylvie analyzed the cover for a few minutes. The model had long, blonde hair, perfect skin and body, and wore a matching pink lace bra and underwear set with tiny bows both between her breasts and above her ... *lady parts* ... Sylvie automatically blushed just trying to think of a word for that area. She was standing with one arm thrown above her head, the other bent with her hand behind her right ear. Her makeup was flawless, head tilted and mouth suggestively open. Sylvie couldn't imagine what situation would call for such a pose in real life, but it would be very alluring if she were lying in bed. Maybe this was the woman she should write about in her romance novel.

With five more minutes until the green rejuvenation mask needed to be washed off, Sylvie slowly started turning the pages, sit-ups forgotten. Holding the magazine above her face, arms half-extended because she was still lying on her back on the floor, left leg crossed over the right, she paged through the pictures near the center first.

Several pages were devoted to the cover model, Gigi, in various outfits, then with parts of outfits, then spread eagle in the centerfold. Sylvie could feel the heat in her face.

Oh my, she doesn't have any hair down there.

Sylvie turned more pages to find a photoshoot of two women, one blonde and one dark-skinned Hispanic, both with fake breasts, taking a shower together. The blonde woman was using the shower wand like a vibrator on the Hispanic woman, who had soap bubbles in various places on her body, although no bubbles covered any of the parts men wanted to see.

Fascinated, and feeling more and more like she didn't know anything of how the world worked, Sylvie turned more pages. She bought the magazine for the naughty letters, but momentarily forgot all about her purpose. The next section featured a couple, the woman obviously in the throes of passion.

"BEEP BEEP BEEP," her phone alarm startled her out of her trance, causing her to drop the *Penthouse* into the green goo on her face, and slam her elbow into the heavy wood coffee table. She looked around the living room guiltily, as if her phone had caught her misbehaving and was going to tell her mother.

Sylvie had a hard time concentrating at work the next day. She had awakened early to check her dating site messages while the coffee brewed, and went straight to *Surfer1968*'s reply.

> Aloha, Sylvie. Sunset would be great. How about Wednesday? I'll bring the wine if you supply the snacks. Let's meet on the airport side of the beach, I'll be driving a black Tacoma. Can't wait to meet you. Jeff.

Sylvie typed out a reply after thinking about it in the shower. Hi Jeff. Wednesday is great. 5:30? Look for me in the brown Ford Ranger. S.

She dressed and looked in the mirror; her skin did look a little rejuvenated from the mask. She wondered what would happen if she used it every night as she grabbed her lunch and drove to work with a smile on her face – she had a date.

After three hours of phone calls and paperwork, at her less-than-exciting job as an accountant, her mind began to drift to her upcoming date. *What am I going to wear?* was the first worry that popped up in her mind. She dialed Colleen's number from her work phone.

"I have a date on Wednesday for sunset at the beach – do I wear a bikini with a cover-up or a cute sundress or shorts and tank top or something that suggests I want him to talk dirty to me?" Sylvie blurted out when she heard Colleen's phone pick up.

"Um, do you want to talk to my mom?" It was Colleen's eight-year-old son.

Sylvie covered the mouthpiece of her phone. "Crap." Speaking again to the boy, she whispered, "Yes, please." She thought of hanging up, but her work number would show on the caller ID. Elbow on desk and head bowed into her hand, covering her eyes, Sylvie waited several long moments for her friend; she knew the boy was telling on her.

"So you're asking my kid for advice now? Sure, he's male, but come on, he's only a kid. He hasn't learned yet that he can Google porn, so I don't think he'll be much help."

"Oh God, I'm so sorry. Why isn't he at school? Why aren't you at work?"

"He has a fever; I just picked him up from school. Mak has meetings all day so I get to do it." Mak, her nickname for Makai, was her husband. "Now what's the problem? From what Sol understands, you need to wear clothes on a date that you can get dirty."

"Well, that's pretty close to the truth. I have a date on Wednesday, at Salt Pond, and I can't figure out how I should look. Cute? Slutty? Shy? Sexy?"

"Shit, Sylvie, maybe I should go on your dates and record them for you to watch later. That would add a nice twist to my marriage. Why are you stressing so much? Wear something sexy but comfortable. Not skin tight, since you'll probably be slouched in a beach chair and you've gotten a little soft in the middle lately. How about a bikini with a pareo on top? Jump in the water before he gets there, dry off, then the pareo will only stick to your tits and ass with your wet bikini showing through. Shy, sporty, and unintentionally sexy, all in one look. But don't get your hair wet, 'cause you want it perfect for a date. Good? Because I need to get Sol settled into bed. I'll call you when I have more time."

Sylvie decided to take her lunch break early so she could get her mind back on her work. Unpacking her turkey sandwich and apple slices at her desk, she typed "first date snacks" into her search engine. Might as well get it all planned out so I can quit worrying, she thought. The first entry listed the top 10 things you shouldn't eat on a first date. Good information, so Sylvie opened it. Corn, hot wings, soup; the list went on to include seven other items she never would have dreamed of bringing to the beach. So far, so good. The next entry contained 15 sexy foods to eat on a date. Scanning the page with a sly smile, Sylvie copied the link and emailed it to herself with Sexy Foods in the subject line, for later reference. Most of them wouldn't work for a beach date, but she could try them out later or use them in her book. She hadn't thought of a restaurant date as an erotic encounter by itself, but quickly worked up a scenario in her head.

She twirled the spaghetti on her fork, leaving several dripping inches dangling towards her plate. Placing it between her plump, red lips, she slowly sucked the noodles into her mouth, staring suggestively into his eyes.

And splatters red sauce across the front of her low-cut blouse, and probably under her nose as well, when the pasta inevitably flew out of control, Sylvie thought. Checking her computer, she realized spaghetti was on the Do Not Eat list, murmured "Oops, wrong one." She sent herself another email of her favorite foods on the forbidden list and closed that window.

Returning to the sexy food list, she picked out possibilities for Wednesday evening.

Sushi. She could see the arousing possibilities of sushi: wide, open mouth with maybe a little tongue sticking out, licking a drip of sauce from my fingers. *But it might get sandy if it's windy and how would we brush it off? Soy dripping on my clothes. Fumbling chopsticks and dumping an entire piece on my lap. Choking to death when I start to talk with my mouth full.*

"Not sushi."

Shrimp. The article suggested seared shrimp, but cocktail-style would be more appropriate for the occasion. And Costco had platters ready-to-go. Sylvie closed her eyes.

The pink-lace-clad Penthouse model dipped her shrimp in the cocktail sauce, lifted it high in the air; with her head tilted back, mouth open and chest out, her tongue darted out to lick the sauce before she closed her pink lips around it, gently pulling the tail from between her teeth.

She opened another tab on her browser, searched, and found that there was a one-in-fifty chance that *Surfer1968* would be allergic to shellfish. Emergency room visits were required by 76% of them. Even casual contact between lips was enough to cause a reaction. She mentally crossed shrimp off the list until later dates, when she knew more about a person.

I'm getting a cheese and cracker tray, she thought. *Goes well with wine. I gotta get back to work.*

Her days flew by with a flurry of work, a dentist appointment, a trip to Costco for the cheese and cracker tray, and an evening out with coworkers. Sylvie didn't even check the messages on the dating site, even though her email told her she had 16 more. *Let's get through the first date before worrying about more*, she told herself. She applied her green rejuvenating mask again on Tuesday evening as she picked the outfit she would wear for sunset the next day. Digging through a drawer of bikinis, Sylvie chose a bright magenta top and black scrunch bottoms, purposely picked to show a little cheek if they ended up in the water together. She was proud of her ass – small, but nicely shaped. She pulled a light purple pareo from the pile; it would match the bikini top but was light enough to be see-through in the wet areas.

Colleen is a genius.

And just in case he was at the beach first, and wearing something fancier than surf shorts, she pulled out a light purple, flower print sundress. She could slip it on before he even knew she had arrived. Sylvie dumped her selections on the couch, pulled the iron and ironing board from the closet, and proceeded to smooth every visible wrinkle. She washed off her mask when her timer went off, then carefully folded her clothing into a bag; she would go to the beach directly after work tomorrow. She could keep the cheese platter in the break room refrigerator, and remembered to tape a *Do Not Eat Under Penalty of Death* note to the top. Then tearing it off, she replaced it with *Please Don't Eat*. With a smiley face.

Sylvie found paper plates and napkins in a cabinet, and slid them into the bag under her clothes. Trying to envision the date, she suddenly panicked and called Colleen.

"Beach chairs or a blanket?"

"Blanket. It'll make him think of a bed. Have you been practicing in your shoes? Good luck tomorrow." She hung up without further conversation.

Sylvie retrieved the black heels from her bedroom, forgotten during the anxiety of a first date. She wobbled back to her closet, unfolded the ironing board in her living room again, walked back and pulled a large, lightweight cotton picnic blanket from a shelf. It was red with a wave print and didn't match her outfits, but it would have to do for now. She carefully ironed it, hunched over because of the extra three inches of Colleen's shoes. The blanket folded and stashed with her clothes, Sylvie suddenly remembered her notebook; the entire purpose of this date was research for her book, and what good would it do if she had one drink too many and forgot the details? She turned towards her desk, not thinking of the shoes, caught the left stiletto heel in the carpet, and smacked her face on the edge of the ironing board before her hands caught her fall on the floor.

"Fuck."

Sylvie's workday flew by; she was nervous about the date, but thankfully she was too busy to give it much thought. Her short lunch break was interrupted by a call from the front desk – a package had been dropped off for her. Sylvie walked down the stairs, absentmindedly thinking about another set of financial forms a client had forgotten to give her, or maybe receipts from her boss for his business trip. Grace, a short, beautiful Filipino receptionist at the firm, handed her a fat manila envelope; Sylvie curiously ripped it open – and three boxes of condoms tumbled onto the floor of the office. "Oh. My. God."

Grace bent down and retrieved a purple box. "*Trojan Ecstasy Fire & Ice*," she read. "Ooh, these are the ones with the tingly gel." Sylvie grabbed the box and stuffed it back in the envelope. She knelt down to gather the other two but Grace was quicker, reaching out for the orange box, *Charged for Orgasmic Pleasure*. She read the back while

Sylvie replaced the yellow box in the envelope, on which she now saw "*Good luck! C*" written in black magic marker.

"Is there an orgy tonight I wasn't invited to?"

Sylvie couldn't get back to her office fast enough. Colleen worked nearby and must have dropped off the package during her lunch break. Sylvie knew she should have been mad, but she actually felt a bit of relief. She hadn't remembered to buy any, and now she had enough for a year of dates.

At 4:30 she yelled a quick goodbye to her coworkers, some of whom had big grins on their faces; one man gave her two thumbs up.

"Go get 'em!"

She ducked into the bathroom to change into her bikini, repenciled her eyeliner, grabbed the untouched cheese plate from the break room refrigerator, and ran out the door. The drive to Salt Pond was a short 10 minutes, and Sylvie made it to the predetermined spot with half an hour to spare. She looked around but did not see a black Tacoma.

Sylvie put her Ranger in four-wheel-drive and backed onto the sand, stopping 20 feet from the water's edge. The beach was sparsely populated, being a Wednesday evening during the school year. It ran along the shore for about two miles with picnic pavilions at the furthest end to the west. Scrub trees and tall grasses filled the land all the way back to the highway, giving it the feel of a separate island unto itself, with no buildings in sight. She pulled the red blanket from her bag and spread it to its full size, with a little help from a nice breeze. She weighted down the windward corners with her slippers and cell phone at one side and her beach bag at another; she dropped her pareo and walked to the water.

She waded in until she was waist deep, pushed off with her feet, and floated on her stomach, feeling the dust of the workday wash away. The water was warm for October. She only stayed in for a few minutes, then hurried back to her truck to dry off and replace her pareo. She brushed her hair one last time, set out the cheese plate and crackers, and waited for Jeff, *Surfer1968*, to arrive. Her notebook and pen peeked out from under the beach bag, ready to record information for her book.

He arrived at exactly 5:30. His black Tacoma pulled onto the sand next to Sylvie's truck, and she thought her heart would explode from anticipation. What if he was nothing like his picture online, maybe using one from his younger days? What if he was creepy? Or gross? Or missing several teeth? She was beginning to panic as she waited for a first glimpse of him, her pulse racing, and he was probably just sitting in his truck casually uncorking the bottle of wine, feeling lucky he had a hot date. What if he was lacing her glass with rufies? She suddenly wished she had offered to bring the drinks. Another minute passed. Why wasn't he getting out of his truck? Sylvie felt very self-conscious in her cold, wet, nearly see-through pareo; Colleen didn't seem like such a genius now.

Finally the door opened and a man emerged from the truck. Not creepy, not gross, just a regular guy. "Sorry, my daughter was on the phone. She's in her first year of college and calls so rarely that I couldn't hang up. I'm Jeff."

He held out his hand, they shook, and he sat down next to Sylvie on the blanket, placing a cooler behind them. Sylvie eyed him as he reached in the cooler; he looked like his picture and had plenty of teeth. She didn't detect any strange body odors. She calmed down a little. Jeff was wearing black surf shorts and a red t-shirt, both neat and new. He didn't look like the chiseled god she wanted for her book, but he didn't look like a rapist, either.

"Nice to meet you, I'm Sylvie. I hope you don't have any issues with cheese; I forgot to ask what types of food you like."

Don't have any issues with cheese? she thought, *great opening line. Real sexy.*

"No, no cheese issues." Jeff handed Sylvie a clear plastic cup of red wine. "Cheers."

"So you have a daughter in college? Where does she go? Any other kids?"

They made awkward small talk for an hour, sipping wine and eating cheese and crackers. Sylvie remembered to stick out her chest suggestively, once even purposely dropping part of a cracker in her cleavage so he could watch her touch herself. Nothing. The sun reached the horizon and the sky started turning pink, with bits of orange around the puffy white clouds.

As the sun dipped below the water, the sky gloriously aflame, he reached out his tan, muscular arm and tugged at her pareo; the flimsy cotton cover-up floated to the sand, leaving only the thin material of her bikini top separating her erect nipples from his hungry eyes. He took her in his arms, his passion burning like the colors of the sunset, and laid her gently on the ground...

"Sylvie?"

"Oh, sorry. Sunsets make me dreamy." Her face was as pink as the clouds.

"I asked if you wanted a jacket – you look like you're freezing. I can't believe you went swimming and didn't bring warmer clothes."

Jeff obviously saw her nipples, hard from the chilly evening air with very little fabric to cover them, and chose to be a gentleman. *That's nice*, Sylvie thought, *but nothing to take notes about. I should have picked a guy with bad grammar. Maybe he'd take a hint.* She shivered. She was cold.

"No, thanks. I should probably be going anyway. I have an early morning. It was great to meet you. Maybe we can have dinner next time."

Why did I say that? she thought, *I don't want to have dinner with him.*

"Sure. This was nice, I'd love to take you out to dinner. I'll send you a message and we can plan an evening. Good night."

He extended his hand to her. Not even a kiss on the cheek. *What am I doing wrong?* Sylvie sadly wondered.

Jeff replaced the cooler in the back of his truck and drove off, waving one last time. Sylvie packed up her bag and threw it with the sandy beach blanket into her truck; she sat in the driver's seat with her notebook open and poised on her steering wheel, staring at the blank page for a moment before writing.

Date #1 notes: Boring. Totally unsexy. Dressed provocatively and he didn't even notice. Need to pick guy who is not so nice. Learn how to incorporate innuendo into conversation so he understands what I want.

Feeling disappointed, Sylvie drove home. She ignored her phone because she didn't want to tell Colleen that her first date was a failure. She ignored the shiny high heels in her living room because she didn't feel like practicing how to walk sexily. She didn't even shower off the dried saltwater. Sylvie pulled on her oversized cotton penguin-print pajamas, turned on the TV, and fell asleep on the couch watching reruns of *Buffy the Vampire Slayer*.

Sylvie didn't check the dating site the next day; she was still feeling down, and not ready to get excited about another guy or another date. She had had such high expectations of romance and adventure but didn't know how to make them reality. Maybe she wasn't the type of girl to attract that kind of excitement in her life; maybe she was destined to have safe, boring encounters with men. While that wasn't a bad thing, she was sure she could find a great guy for a relationship and still have sparks fly. Her short-term goal was to incorporate a little fantasy into her life to find inspiration for her book. And she was failing.

She called Colleen at lunch, looking for a shoulder to cry on.

"Good God, girl, you went on one freakin' date," Colleen said. "You've only talked to one guy. That's not failure, that's laziness. Write to 10 guys at once; there's no one to be faithful to. Go out to bars after work. Go to church – if you watch the news you know that some of the kinkiest freaks are religious, they just deny it until they're caught. Quit stressing, keep practicing with your shoes, and get your ass out there. It's a cute ass – I know you'll find someone who wants to spank it."

Sylvie knew Colleen spoke the truth, but it didn't help her feel any better. She moped around the office, and no one dared ask her about her date or if she had a chance to use her collection of condoms, which was the best company gossip in a long time. After lunch, she drove to her bank to make some deposits for the company. The line was long and Sylvie stood there silently with unfocused eyes, not making the usual small talk with her neighbors in line. After a few minutes, she came back to herself and realized where her eyes rested – on the muscular, blue-jean-clad backside of the construction worker in front of her.

His jeans were dirty, faded and perfectly cupped his ass. Brown steel-toed boots, a loose t-shirt full of holes, and a dusty baseball cap completed the outfit. Sylvie was certain that if she leaned any closer towards him, he would smell like sweat and sawdust. His brown hair fell almost to the middle of his back, an inch shorter than hers, and tattoos snaked out of his sleeves down his well-formed tan arms.

She walked down the busy street after work, tense from a long day. Passing a construction site, she glanced toward the unfinished building and caught the eye of the last worker finishing up for the day. He dropped his toolbox when he saw her; her thin minidress, catching the breeze, showed her bronzed thighs and a flash of her pink thong. She kept watching him and didn't try to tame her errant skirt – her eyes invited him to ask for more. With long strides of muscular legs, he strode towards her, dropping his orange hard hat along the way. Stepping over the yellow caution tape to the sidewalk, his tough, work-stained hand reached behind to the small of her back and roughly pulled her close – her head flung back and her arms instinctively reaching out for balance around his bulging shoulders. She looked up into his icy blue eyes and he pressed his lips to hers, urgently, crushing her to his body. She could feel his...

"Sylvie!"

"Wake up, girl! You ready?"

Abashed at her thoughts, Sylvie walked to the open teller with a flushed face. She looked around for the construction worker and saw him at the next window; he was looking at her, wondering who was being called. He was as hot from the front as he was from behind.

Talk to him! she yelled at herself, *Say hello! Give him your phone number! Tell him he's got a nice ass! Be that flirty girl! This is the guy from the fantasy!*

She blankly stared back, opened her mouth, and nothing came out. After a moment's pause, he turned back to his business, collected his money and receipt, and walked out of the bank. Sylvie sighed deeply, feeling a failure again, and sadly pulled the checks from her bag.

"He's hot, yeah?" the teller asked. "If I weren't married…"

"Do you know him? Is he single?"

"He comes in here every Thursday. Super nice guy. His name is Michael. I think he broke up with his girlfriend a few weeks ago. Do you want me to give him your number? I can let all the girls know. You two would look good together, and I could see you staring at his ass."

Sylvie still had a blank stare on her face. "Uh, yes. Please." She reached into her purse and pulled her card from her wallet. Taking the bank pen, attached by chain to the counter, she scribbled her mobile number on the back, wrote *Call me*, and signed her name. She handed it to the teller, finished her work, and drove back to the office. *Colleen would be proud of me, arranging to get him my business card*, she thought. *I just won't tell her that I froze instead of speaking to him directly.*

After her bank encounter, Sylvie had a renewed outlook on her project. He was hot, and he had looked at her. He really looked – but she froze. She could have made it happen, and that's what mattered. A small smile crept onto her face, and she decided to pour extra time and effort into her research. She could make this work. For the book.

That evening, she logged onto the dating site for the first time in days. Colleen's advice had been to communicate with several guys at once, so Sylvie began. She had 36 unread messages.

She started with her "Maybe" list, and wrote to *Goodlife_49*.

> Aloha! When will you be visiting? I'm always looking for adventures, maybe we can hike to a secluded beach for a dip.

Sylvie thought her response was suggestive enough. She hoped it was.

The others on her "Maybe" list seemed boring after her first date – now she knew what she was looking for. She deleted them, changed her filter to "Not looking for a serious relationship," and scrolled through the new messages; this time she was looking for incorrect spelling and sexy pictures.

Giz.Allday wrote, those shoes are HAWT lets hang out

No punctuation whatsoever. Horrible screen name. Only 5'8" but looks great in surf shorts. No other information. Winner.

Sylvie typed, I'm in. I'll wear the shoes. You look scrumptious.

She wondered if he knew what *scrumptious* meant.

Phred69 wrote, Hey girl, I'd like to check you out. Why don't we get some cocktails?

Sylvie shuddered. His pictures were good, several of him hiking at overlooks along the Na Pali coast. No kids, didn't smoke, wasn't looking for a relationship, explorer. Why not?

Hi Phred, she refused to add the 69. I'd love to explore you over cocktails. What day is good?

AceLover only had one picture on his profile, a selfie at the gym – one bicep flexed, the other arm holding his phone near his face, headphones extending into his ears. He was almost handsome but wore a soul patch, which made him look like a douchebag when combined with the pose. Cocky. Perfect.

You're shy, I'm not. I love working out and my black lab. You look like you work out let's hit the gym together. My name is Marcus.

Sylvie wrote back, Hi Marcus. Get me a day pass at your gym and we'll get sweaty together.

She opened the other messages, only to look at the profile pictures, and decided she was done. Four replies was the most Sylvie could write in one sitting. She hadn't anticipated how much mental energy it took to wade through messages and dumb herself down enough to seem like all she wanted to do was get laid. She hoped her replies gave that impression.

Sylvie eyed the list of messages one last time before deleting and noticed a new one from *Surfer1968*.

> Sylvie it was so great to meet you. I'd love to take you to dinner, give me a call.

And included his phone number. *Delete*.

She closed the computer with a smile on her face, and went looking for Colleen's shoes.

Sylvie set her alarm half an hour earlier on Friday to allow enough time to read messages before work. She jumped out of bed at the sound, unusual for her, and practically ran to the kitchen. The coffee was nearly done brewing as Sylvie had set the timer the night before. She poured soy milk in her waiting mug and yanked the pot from the machine. Drips of coffee sprayed the counter as she filled the mug, which normally would call for an instantaneous sanitizing of her entire kitchen counter with a Clorox wipe, but the mess was overlooked in anticipation of what awaited her on her computer. She opened it and logged onto the dating site, bouncing up and down on her chair and spilling more coffee.

No new messages.

Sylvie slowly showered and dressed for work.

The workday crawled by slowly, but Sylvie didn't dare log in to check for messages on her work computer. She knew enough about the IT department to know it was unlikely someone would see, but she wasn't prepared to explain to Human Resources why she was dating online during work hours. She made an excuse to go to the bank to look for the hot construction worker, but ended up disappointed. Friday night was closing in and she had no plans, so she accepted an invitation to join Grace at the bar next door for an after-work cocktail.

One drink, Sylvie told herself, *then I'll go home and see if I have plans for the rest of the weekend.* But she brought her notebook along, just in case.

She spotted Grace sitting at an outdoor table, talking to the waitress. Sylvie slid onto the bench beside her, facing the ocean and a few tables away from the band, just as Grace was finishing her order.

"I'd like a glass of dark rum with some ice," Sylvie added. "Did you order any food?"

"I got us calamari and pork nachos, is that ok?"

"Perfect." Sylvie wondered how those rated on the sexy foods list.

"Tell me about your date! You didn't look happy on Thursday, but that doesn't tell me whether you used the tingly condoms or not. Could've been bad sex."

"There was no sex. No tingly condoms. He was nice but it was boring."

"So you aren't going to see him again?"

"Probably not." As an afterthought, Sylvie added, "Any hot, single guys in your life? Maybe I just need a fling." She wasn't going to let Grace in on her secret.

"No one comes to mind right away. Let me think about it. I'm sure we can find someone you'd like."

Three more coworkers joined Sylvie and Grace at the table, drinks arrived, additional drinks were ordered, and discussion of available men was forgotten in the chatter of work gossip. Sylvie knew that everyone wanted to know about her date. It was a hot topic at work, but she didn't volunteer any information to the group; they could find out from Grace after she left.

Sometime during her second glass of dark rum, Sylvie's mind wandered away from the conversation as she looked around the bar. It was crowded, typical for a Friday night after work. She waved to several people she knew and watched the band return from a break. It was a local band playing a mix of radio hits and their own creations. They began the next set with Stevie Wonder's *Superstitious*, the ukulele adding a unique sound, which got some of the crowd onto their feet and made the rest bounce on their seats.

The lead singer had a great voice and moved well in the small space set aside for the band. He was wearing surf shorts and a t-shirt, and Sylvie found him very attractive.

The stadium erupted as the singer approached the front of the stage, falling to his knees as he hit the high notes. She was in the front row, surrounded by a mass of screaming people. Her high heels made her stand tall above the crowd, and smiling and singing along, she caught his eye. He froze for a moment, thunderstruck, as he stared at her, then reached out for her hand as the guitar solo began. "Help me out, people!" he yelled into the mic, and her neighbors lifted her as he pulled her up onto the stage. She stumbled, and he caught her tightly in his arms, instantly soaking the front of her flimsy, white dress with sweat. They stared into each other's eyes, the roar of the crowd fading away until it was just the two of them in their world. "You are the most beautiful woman I've ever seen," he whispered, his lips lightly grazing the outer edge of her ear, sending waves of desire through her body. "I have to have you right now." Dropping the mic, he picked her up in his muscular arms and carried her backstage while the band continued to play. One of her shoes fell to the ground, but neither of them noticed; they were only aware of the intense burning for...

"Sylvie! Are you coming or not?"

She jumped, spilling the remainder of her drink, as Grace shook her arm.

"Huh? What? Sorry, I was really into that song." She noticed that the band was silent, deciding what to play next. "Oh."

"Charlie and Susan have to leave for dinner and I'm due at home. Are you staying?"

"No, I've got a big day tomorrow. I'm gonna head home." She noticed that the check was on the table; Sylvie calculated her share, slid her money into the black folder with the rest, and walked to the parking lot in a daze.

Sylvie powered up her computer before stripping off her work clothes. In panties and bra, she put on Colleen's shoes, runway-walked to the bathroom, and applied the green mask to her face. She picked up the *Playboy* magazine from her coffee table on her way back to the kitchen and tore off the prohibitive plastic covering, revealing a cover model in a strategically ripped white hoodie, leaning on gymnast's rings. Her lower body was naked and gleaming with oil, the torn sweatshirt revealing all but her nipples from the side. Sylvie sighed, tossed the magazine back onto the table, and slowly lowered herself onto the beige carpet. Face up and high heels in the air, she counted down the first set of sit-ups, silently promising herself that she'd get up early the next morning and go for a run and swim.

Completing four sets of sit-ups, Sylvie rolled to her stomach for pushups, doing six before dropping to her knees. Thankfully, her mask timer went off soon after, and she catwalked back to the bathroom to rinse.

At the kitchen table, Sylvie logged onto the dating site and checked her messages. Three replies, and four new messages. She clicked on the first one, from *Giz.Allday*. No words, just an attachment. She clicked on the link.

It was a picture of an erect penis.

"Ach, really?" Sylvie cried out in surprise.

After looking away in disgust, she peeked at the picture from the corner of her eye, nose wrinkled as if it smelled bad. *Who would send this?* she wondered, amazed at his nerve. Amazed at the size, now that she was curious and looked closer. The head was huge and purple, and seemed very angry. She had seen a number of penises in her time, none of which were very pretty, but this was just gross. She could see a hand grasping beneath the balls, squishing them, making sure the penis was pointed at the camera.

"Ech." *Delete*.

She clicked on the next message. *Goodlife_49* wrote, I'll be there in two weeks. I'd love to check out a secret beach with you. I'll send a message before I leave.

Okay, good, I have two weeks to make a plan for him. I'll ask Colleen for help, she thought.

She replied, Can't wait to meet you. Pack your shorts and hiking shoes, but you may not need the shorts. Smiley face.

The third message was from *Phred69*. Can you meet Saturday night?

Sylvie replied that she could, at 7 p.m., at Keoki's, and she would be wearing a red dress with black heels.

Four new messages, all of which were from middle-aged, boring-looking men, politely asking for a date. *Delete*.

Sylvie catwalked off to bed.

Sylvie woke up on Saturday determined to get some research done on her new book. She had high hopes for her date, and hummed to herself as she drank coffee and dressed for her run. The day was breezy and cloudless, so she packed a bikini and towel for a swim, applied sunscreen, and drove to the beach.

She pulled into the parking lot near the beach, traded her flip-flops for socks and running shoes, clipped on her iPod, started her GPS watch, and set out to run for an hour. At the half-way point, three miles away from her truck, she wished she hadn't been so ambitious; her last run was a month ago. Sylvie turned around and began walking back, hoping someone she recognized drove by so she could catch a ride.

Finally back at the beach after a combination of walking and jogging, Sylvie changed into her bikini for a short swim to cool down. Her eyes scanned the light Saturday morning crowd for friends, coworkers, or hot men she should find an excuse to meet while wearing a bikini. Not seeing anyone to talk to, she waded into the water, adjusted her goggles, and swam for 20 minutes. The water was clear and the reef was alive with fish of all colors, mostly groups of bright yellow butterfly fish and trigger fish guarding their territory.

Emerging from the ocean, Sylvie spotted Mak, Colleen's husband, setting up a shade tent in the sand. Sol and his younger sister, Lily, were chasing each other around a pile of chairs and towels waiting to be set up. Colleen was approaching with two large bags of toys and snorkel gear, and a cooler. It was a family beach day, and Sylvie was excited to run into her adopted family.

"Sylvie! I left a message on your phone a few minutes ago to meet us here. Hope you can stay for a while."

At the sound of her mother's voice talking to Sylvie, Lily ran over and grabbed Sylvie's hand, dragging her back towards the ocean. They always swam together.

"Lily, come back! I need to sunscreen you before you go in the water."

Sylvie was thankful for a moment to relax before playing with the children. She loved them, but it took a few minutes to mentally prepare for the constant attention they expected from her. Plus, she wanted to talk to Colleen about her date that evening, and Lily was too young to understand, as long as she spelled the important words. She followed Lily up the beach to where Colleen was waiting with a large tube of spf 50 sunblock, already squirted into her hand.

"I have a date tonight," she said as Colleen rubbed the white paste on Lily's back. "We're meeting for cocktails, and I'm going to wear my red dress with your shoes. I'm nervous."

"There's no point in being nervous; that just ruins all the fun. It's not like this is the man of your dreams, right? Show up early, have a drink or two before he gets there, and be bold. Only if he's worth it, of course."

Colleen's children were lucky, Sylvie thought. They were growing up learning a whole lot more about the world much faster than she did.

"I sincerely doubt he's the man of my dreams. His screen name has s-i-x-t-y-n-i-n-e in it. This is just for the book."

"Sixty-nine," Lily squealed, jumping up and down. "I'm the best speller in my class!"

Sylvie saw Mak shaking his head, with a small smile on his face. "Sylvie, maybe you and Colleen should go have a private chat. I'll watch the kids."

"No need, it's a family day. Let's play." And Sylvie ran back to the ocean, both children right behind her.

Sylvie returned home exhausted, happy, and a little sunburnt after spending the better part of the day at the beach with Colleen's family. She had five hours until her date, and used the first one for a nap.

Waking refreshed and feeling great from a day of exercise and sun, Sylvie took a long shower, putting extra care into shaving her legs; she didn't want to show up with fresh cuts around her ankles or knees. She smoothed verbena lotion over her body in anticipation of a man's hands touching all those places. She knew she was going to wear her favorite red dress, worn only on very special occasions, but what to wear under it was a problem. She dug through her underwear drawer, pulling out every possibility and throwing them on her bed. Nothing matched. In frustration, she wondered how she got to be her age and didn't own a matching bra and pantie set. She didn't have time to go to the mall, so she had to do the best she could for tonight and hope it was dark if he did happen to see her undressing.

Sylvie picked basic black to wear under her dress, the closest she could get to matching, and decided to remedy her problem immediately. As she walked to her computer, she saw the *Penthouse* magazine on her coffee table; adorning the nymphet on the cover was the pink lace lingerie with little bows which was what she needed for her next date. Mad that she hadn't thought of this earlier, Sylvie opened her browser, typed *Victoria's Secret* into the search bar, and started shopping.

Sylvie found a parking space outside Keoki's at 6 o'clock, an hour before the promised time to meet *Phred69*; enough time to have a drink and rehearse the things she wanted to talk about. After purchasing two sets of sexy, matching underwear and a naughty-looking sheer red teddy, Sylvie had looked for conversation tips online and jotted them down in her notebook, which was tucked in her oversized black purse. She had read them over and over while she got dressed and applied her makeup, almost like she was cramming for a college exam, but worried she would be too nervous to remember.

What would be so wrong about treating this exactly like the cheaters in school? she had asked herself, and decided to ink microscopic reminders on the underside of her left wrist to aid her memory.

The notes were simple, only key words to ideas she needed to incorporate into the evening. *Touch* meant she should reach out and touch his arm or knee on occasion; *gaze*, to look into his eyes; *hair* so she remembered to twirl her hair around her finger, or maybe suggestively stick the ends into her mouth and suck on it. The list only covered a few square inches and she was certain *Phred69* wouldn't notice.

The restaurant was crowded, but Sylvie managed to find a single seat at the rectangular bar. She wasn't exactly sure what her date looked like – the one detail she had forgotten to etch into her mind – but she knew he'd find her in her red dress and heels; she was the only woman so dressed up. After ordering a glass of tequila with ice to calm her nerves, she applauded herself for her flawless walk from the truck to her current seat; Sylvie had walked barefoot from her house, only donning the stilettos upon arrival in the parking lot. She had pictured the runway model in her mind again and sashayed across the blacktop in what she thought was a similar manner. And it had worked – she didn't wobble or trip over anything, which she took as a good omen for the evening.

Sylvie reached for a menu to decide in advance what she should order; while sitting with her date she would pretend to be indecisive, but now she wanted to think through all the possibilities and choose a dish containing only foods from the sexy list. She didn't want anything to drip on her dress or leave gobs of green in her teeth.

"You look a little low there," the bartender said, bringing Sylvie out of her study of the menu. The bartender, tall and slim with an adorable, unlined face, was pointing at her drink. "Another?"

"Yes, please. One more can't hurt." Sylvie slyly glanced at her wrist notes, saw *smile* and *touch*, and lightly grazed the bartender's hand with her fingers as he reached for her glass, smiling at him. His hand momentarily froze, he looked into her eyes, smiled back, and retrieved her glass for a refill.

Oh my God, it works! she silently exclaimed to herself. *I can do this!*

Half an hour before her date, Sylvie started on her second tequila. The shot was much more generous than the first, and came with a sexy smile from the bartender as it was served. Sylvie practically fell off her stool with excitement.

Returning her attention to the menu, she decided on the sashimi for her dinner; without rice, the mouthfuls wouldn't be too big to be messy or choke on, and she could strategically drip some soy sauce onto her fingers and lick it off while gazing into his eyes. The evening was looking better and better as she finished her second drink, listening to the music.

It was last call and she was the only patron left in the restaurant. The bartender slid the check towards her, letting his fingers linger on the paper until she read the words he had handwritten, "I paid your tab and I'd like to take you home." She glanced up and their eyes met; she smiled her consent – words were not necessary. Suddenly alive with desire, she boldly slid off her stool and walked to meet him body to body, with no bar between them. His strong hands gripped her waist and lifted her onto the bar, sliding his hands down to the small of her back, pressing his face between her breasts, taking in her essence. He tilted his head upwards and kissed her neck, her head falling backward, eyes closed. She wrapped her legs around him and pulled him close as he slid his hands up her back and slowly pulled the zipper of her dress all the way down. His fingertips on the bare skin of her back sent shivers straight to her core, and she knew she had to have him immediately, right there, on the bar. She shrugged her shoulders and her dress fell to her waist, revealing her breasts, nipples erect in anticipation of his tongue and lips. She didn't have to wait long – his hungry mouth found its way to a sweet spot as his fingers unclasped her bra and gently pulled the red lace away from…

A tap on her shoulder reminded Sylvie that she was at the bar to meet her date, causing her to startle out of her daydream.

"Sylvie?"

"Yes…"

"I'm Fred. Nice dress. Do you want to stay at the bar or find a table?"

Sylvie noticed the seat to the right of her was now vacant. "Let's stay right here." She smiled in anticipation as she envisioned flirting with both men, and having her choice at the end of the evening.

Fred took his seat, and Sylvie swiveled to get a better look at him. She could tell he wasn't as tall as her, but he was tan and in good shape, presumably from all the hiking he mentioned in his profile. He had all his teeth – *thank God* – and while he wasn't exactly handsome, he wasn't bad looking, either – short, brown hair with the slightest touch of curl over soft brown eyes.

Sylvie's nerves kicked in again as they ordered a round of drinks, Sylvie's third in an hour. Her mind seemed to empty of all the conversation tips, so she quickly peeked at her wrist as Fred was facing the bartender, ordering a beer. She wasn't quick enough, though.

"Is that a tattoo? Can I see?"

Sylvie slammed her arm down onto the bar in embarrassment. "No, I scratched myself earlier and I was checking on it, that's all." But she had managed to glimpse the word *him*, reminding herself to ask about him and look very interested in what he was saying.

"I saw your hiking pictures online; you seem to get out quite a bit. What else do you do?"

"I got laid off from my job about a year ago and I haven't really found anything else yet."

"Oh. It's so expensive to live here, have you been able to get unemployment for so long?"

"Well, I wasn't technically laid off so I never qualified for unemployment. I was living with my girlfriend at the time, but we broke up and I moved back in with my parents, ya know, to help them out a bit."

"Oh."

A few moments of awkward silence followed as Sylvie pondered the idea of getting involved with a middle-aged man who lived with his parents. She mentally shook her head, *it's just for sex!* she reminded herself. *I don't have to give him my phone number!*

"What do you do for a living? There weren't many details on your profile."

"I'm an accountant."

"I bet that makes good money. Where do you work?"

She stared into his eyes, her mind screaming, *don't tell him! Don't tell him!* and risked a fast glance at her wrist's cheat sheet to help her turn the conversation back to him. Sylvie had placed her arm next to her glass, and the condensation on the bar had smeared the words into a runny blob that was slowly inching its way towards her elbow.

She instinctively hid her arm on her lap and thought hard for another word on her list: *Hair*.

Sylvie inserted her right index finger into her hair and began twirling; Fred was still staring at her in expectation of her answer.

Smile. It was coming back to her now. *Compliment*.

Sylvie fixed what she felt was a warm smile on her face, "I can tell that hiking keeps you in great shape. You look very strong."

With her ink-stained arm in her lap and her right hand twirling in her hair, Sylvie regretfully realized she had no way to sip her drink. Fred smiled at the compliment and began to talk about his explorations.

"I try to get out of the house every day, ya know, the parents and all, so I've checked out all the hikes on the island. I bet no one knows the trails around here better than I do. I bet I've gone through 10 pairs of hiking boots this year."

Sylvie started to reach for her drink but her hand wouldn't move – she had nervously twirled her hair into a knot around her ring.

"What's your favorite?" She tugged her hand some more, silently pleading with her ring to let go.

"There's a trail along the coast I really like, it's a pretty hardcore climb, about six miles, but it's got ocean views the whole way. Totally worth it. The other day I was up there and saw this great big…" He narrowed his eyes as he looked at her more closely. "Are you okay?"

Sylvie was not. She didn't want Fred to see her ink-smudged left arm, but she needed it to get her right hand free of her knotted hair. The dilemma was written all over her face.

"Oh it's nothing, just my hand is stuck," Sylvie said as nonchalantly as she could. "What were you saying about the trail? It sounds so beautiful. Tell me more about things you like to do."

Fred didn't take the conversational bait. "Your hand is stuck? On what?"

Feeling like she had no other choice, and now desperately wanting to chug her drink to forget her embarrassment, Sylvie lifted her left arm off her lap to free her ring, runny, black ink plainly in sight down her arm and imprinted onto the front of her dress. She pulled the ring off her finger and left it dangling in her piece of snarled hair while she took a long, slow sip of tequila.

"Uh, do you need some help… with… that…?" Fred shyly pointed at the ring in her hair.

"No, I got it." Sylvie reached out once again with her blackened arm and began to untangle the mess, tipping a bit tipsily on her stool as the tequila finally hit her and smudging ink on her right cheek.

"Uh, you got…"

"I know," she snapped, wondering how the night had taken such a bad turn so quickly.

"Ok, um," Fred chugged the remainder of his beer. "I'm gonna get going. You look like you might wanna, uh, go home. Uh …"

He turned and walked to the exit, as fast as he could without running.

And without paying for his beer.

Freeing the ring and finishing the rest of her drink, Sylvie crossed her arms on the bar and rested her forehead on them, absently staring at Colleen's black shoes.

"Are you ready for another?" The hot bartender was clearly speaking to her. Sylvie lifted her head, ink-stained and tangled, "Just the check, please."

"I can't do this again. Last night was a disaster. He was middle-aged, unemployed and living with his parents, but I was the loser." Sylvie was sitting at her kitchen table in the exact position she was last in at the bar, arms on table, forehead on arms; her empty coffee cup sitting next to her phone, which was set on speaker.

"Oh honey, you know you're not a loser. It was just a bad night, it happens. Forget about it and move on." Colleen had laughed for several minutes while Sylvie described her date on the previous evening, and was still having trouble keeping her giggles under control.

"I can't I can't I can't. I can't do it again. I don't care about writing a stupid book, I'm an accountant. I don't know what I was thinking."

"Yes, you can. I know how much this means to you, and you're a good writer. You just need some help with life. At least you had a bad night with a guy you weren't interested in. And will never see again. Did he say anything online?"

"I didn't look. He probably either blocked me or is telling everyone I'm crazy. I don't care. I'm done."

"Really, Sylvie," Colleen actually snorted out a held-in laugh and had to move the phone from her mouth for a moment. "You've been on two dates in the last week. In the last year, actually. It takes time to get your confidence back and you're taking this way too seriously. If you'd just relax and treat these guys like the booty calls you're looking for, I think it would be much easier. Why are you wasting so much energy trying to impress them? You're hot. End of story. Get laid and write about it. Now drag your ass to the beach and go for a swim; you'll feel much better. We're headed there as soon as I can get my little monkeys ready. Why don't you meet us?"

"Ehh, fine. Whatever. See you in an hour." Sylvie didn't even bother to hang up her phone, just sat at her table with her head down, wishing she could stay like that all day.

But a day in the sun and ocean did Sylvie a lot of good. She swam by herself for an hour, and being immersed in the chilly water helped curb her feelings of inadequacy; her mind was occupied by the wonder of the underwater life all around her. She only stopped when she spotted a baby eagle ray in the bay, then swam to the beach to fetch Sol and Lily, towing along boogie boards in case they tired so far from shore. They marveled at the ray, which swam beneath them for ten minutes before gliding away to deeper water.

Sylvie lay on her beach towel next to Colleen, listening to the latest drama in her kids' lives; Sol had a crush on a girl in his class and was adamant about bringing her a flower every day.

"He sure didn't get his romantic tendencies from his father," Colleen joked. "It's been years since I've seen a flower I didn't buy for myself."

Lily had decided she only wanted to eat dinosaur-shaped chicken nuggets at every meal, and would starve herself if none were offered.

"I got a note home from school the other day about how unhealthy her packed lunches are, and how I should be more concerned with my daughter's nutrition. I'd love to see her teacher try to change her mind. That girl is so stubborn. Maybe I should go on some dates for you, and you can deal with these lunatic children I have. I swear, we couldn't have been like that as kids. I don't know where they get these ideas."

Sylvie enjoyed an afternoon pleasantly spent with her friends, but she had to go home and deal with the aftermath of the previous night and prepare for a new week of work.

"How do you get ink out of a dress?" she hated to bring it up, since Colleen immediately grinned and had to wait a moment before replying to get her face under control.

"Throw it out and buy a new one."

The first thing Sylvie saw on her desk Monday morning was a pink sticky note from Grace, stuck on the center of her computer screen. *Come see me ASAP!!*

"Oh, God," Sylvie thought. "What could possibly have happened over the weekend that is so important?"

She took her time putting her lunch away and sorting through a stack of mail before walking down the stairs to find Grace. Sylvie had to wait a moment while Grace transferred a phone call.

"Good morning. I saw your note. What's going on?"

Grace was bubbling with enthusiasm, bouncing as she talked. "I found the guy for you! He's perfect! He just moved here for work, and my husband brought him to dinner last night. He's an engineer of some sort, I can't really remember. Smart, tall, pretty good looking; I told him all about you and gave him your phone number. You need to meet him! His name is Russ and I'm so sure you guys will hit it off!"

The expression on Sylvie's face hadn't changed from her polite work demeanor, and Grace noticed.

"I'm serious, you'll love him. Please, just give him a chance?"

"I don't know, Grace, I haven't been too lucky with my love life lately. I'd hate for something awkward to happen, then I couldn't hang out with you after work if you brought him along." Sylvie did not want to involve her work life with her research, and was not feeling romantically inclined at the moment.

"Oh please, please go out with him, just once? I'm sure you'll change your mind when you meet him. He's a really great guy."

"I'll think about it. If he calls."

Sylvie dove into her work, trying to keep her mind off romance. Thankfully, it was a busy day and she didn't need to look for distractions; Russ was all but forgotten when it was time to go home, until she ran into Grace on her way out.

"You promise you'll give him a chance?"

"I promise I'll listen to his voicemail if he calls." That was the most she was prepared to offer.

Sylvie didn't check the dating site again for four days. She kept her mind on work, went to the beach to swim, and cleaned her house. She made several attempts at writing her romance novel, but was continuously frustrated by her lack of imagination.

In the middle of the day on Thursday, Sylvie remembered it was the usual day Michael, the construction worker, went to the bank. She couldn't find any reason to go herself but made an effort to keep an eye on her mobile phone in case he called. She knew the gossip-loving women at the bank wouldn't fail to give him her business card, and small waves of excitement ran through her as she thought about meeting him. Behind her closed eyes she could see his perfect ass in his work-stained jeans, and his muscular, tattooed arms; she wondered what his voice sounded like; probably deep and sexy and confident. He looked like a take-charge kind of guy, that's exactly what she needed.

She closed her eyes and tried to remember his lips, and what they might feel like when he kissed her.

Maybe because she was willing it to happen with her thoughts, her mobile phone rang. Startled, Sylvie fumbled for the phone and knocked a stack of paperwork onto the floor; without a second glance at the mess she made, she accepted the call, "Hello?"

"Sylvie?"

The voice was not exactly how she had heard it in her mind – it was slightly higher than she imagined, and lacking the supreme confidence she had already attributed to Michael.

"Yes, this is Sylvie." Her heart was racing.

"I was given your phone number, and normally I don't call women without meeting them first, but I was assured that we would get along very well, so I'm calling to ask you out on a date. I hope you were told good things about me, too."

"Oh, I was! And I was hoping you'd call. I'd love to go out with you."

"Excellent. I was a little worried that Grace hadn't told you. I'm new to the island and I'm anxious to get to know more people."

Sylvie's heart sunk.

"This is…?"

"Russ. Russ Templeton. I was transferred here for work about two weeks ago and I have to admit, it's been a little rough. I've lived in Boise my whole life, and I had to leave all my friends, but the opportunity was too good to pass up. So here I am, ready to get started with my new life and find new friends."

Sylvie was so disappointed she couldn't think of anything to say, causing several silent moments to pass.

"I was given a couple tickets for a boat trip on Sunday, and I was going to ask one of the guys from work, but figured it would be a great way to see the sights while we get to know each other. Are you free on Sunday?"

"Sure, I can do Sunday. Listen, I have to get back to work," Sylvie lied. "I have a meeting in a few minutes. Text me the info and I'll meet you there."

"Great. It was nice talking to you, and I'm looking forward to the trip."

"Yeah, me too."

Once again, Sylvie found herself with her head down on her arms, staring at her feet.

After a quick dip in the ocean to wash away the work day, Sylvie started dinner and opened her laptop to check messages from the online dating site. Thirteen new messages and three replies; after stirring the bubbling tomato sauce on the stove, she turned down the heat to simmer, put a pot of water on for pasta, let out a deep sigh, and clicked on the first reply.

Giz.Allday wrote, Ya know ya want it.
Delete. Block user.

AceLover was more polite. I'm all for getting sweaty! I'll be at the gym on Saturday morning! Meet me there at 7! Let me know! Excited to pump iron with you!

He ended with the address for the gym.

So many exclamation points, Sylvie thought, *is that the sign of a steroid user?* She replied, See you at 7.

She smiled to herself; even if the date was horrible she'd get in a nice workout before her bikini date on Sunday with Russ.

The final reply was from *Goodlife_49*. I arrive a week from Friday, and I'm just checking in to make sure we're still on. Maybe we can meet up on Sunday after I've had a chance to settle in. I'm afraid I don't know much about the island so I'm hoping you can pick a good spot for us. I'm open to anything.

Sylvie didn't bother to make any sexual innuendos when she wrote back. *A fairly intelligent-sounding guy*, Sylvie thought. *It'll either happen or it won't, no sense in making a fool of myself before we meet*. She replied, I have a great place picked out, hope you're up for a hike and swim. I've got you on my calendar for next Sunday.

She made another mental note to ask Colleen about possible locations for the date. Sylvie hadn't ventured very far from home or work in a while and had forgotten the fun places couples went for privacy on the beach. It had been far too long since she had someone to go with.

Sylvie stirred the sauce and added noodles to the boiling water before sitting back down to read the thirteen new messages. With a quick glance at the list, she clicked on *Footworshipper* first.

> It would be my extreme pleasure to honor you and your gorgeous feet like you deserve. Share a drink with me as you soak your feet in a warm bath. After that, I'll rub them with lotion and gently ease them back into your heels. If you like, I have quite a selection of women's shoes that are available for you to try. I'm also quite fond of painting nails and have several colors to choose from, although the red in your picture is stunning. It looks like *Aphrodite*, one of my favorites. Treat yourself to a night with me, you won't regret it.

Sylvie sat for a moment, just staring at her computer screen with her mouth open. After she reread the message twice more, she copied and pasted it into an email to send to Colleen. Then she grabbed her phone and texted *email* to Colleen, so she'd look for it.

Sylvie decided she'd read the remainder of her messages another time, her spaghetti was ready and she wanted to end her foray into the dating site on a fun note.

As she sat down in her living room to eat, Colleen texted back. *Yes! Free pedicure! Ask him if I can come too!* She had attached a picture of her feet.

Friday came and went, and even though she had promised herself she wouldn't worry, Sylvie began to feel the anxiety of meeting a new man for her date in the morning. The moment she arrived home from work, she began ripping items of clothing out of her closet and flinging them onto her bed. Sports bras, tank tops, running shorts, yoga pants, ankle socks, underwear – Sylvie was surprised at how much workout wear she owned that had been hidden in her closet. She grabbed four pairs of shoes from the closet floor and lined them in a row along the foot of the bed; should she pick the shoes she wanted to wear, then match her outfit to them? Or, should she pick out her shirt first? In a bout of indecision as to where to start, Sylvie headed to the bathroom to apply a coat of the green rejuvenation mask to her face while she thought. And as long as she was doing "date maintenance," as she had recently begun to think of it, she should practice in the heels as well.

Finding Colleen's shoes in the living room, Sylvie sat to slide them on her feet, trying to imagine *Footworshipper* kneeling in front of her like a man selling her the pair in a shoe store. She smiled to herself and wondered if she had the courage to meet up with him and try something new. Sylvie catwalked to the kitchen and poured herself a glass of tequila; maybe after a drink she'd reply to him.

As she headed back to the bedroom, the *Playboy* magazine caught her eye, showing the hot blonde model in the ripped sweatshirt leaning on the gymnast rings. A gym picture. And she was headed for a gym date the next day. She hadn't explored the magazine yet, and maybe there was something in it to give her an idea of what to wear for her date in the morning. Sylvie sat on her couch with her drink and slowly flipped the pages to the middle section where the model was featured. The first pictures showed the gleaming, oiled woman leaning on the rings, similar to the cover.

Fake boobs, Sylvie thought. *I'm not sure mine would be so attractive in a ripped shirt if I wasn't wearing a bra.*

With the first sips of tequila warming her, and no dinner, Sylvie thought she should at least explore the possibility. She turned the pages to view the entire center spread, "Oh my, does *anyone* have hair down there?" she asked aloud to the magazine. She removed Colleen's high heels and set out to recreate the centerfold photo. Grabbing a pair of scissors from her desk, refilling her glass of tequila, stripping down to her panties, and lacing her bright pink

Nikes onto her feet, Sylvie chose a loose running shirt she hadn't worn in months and began to cut. First, she hemmed it to fall just under her breasts. Next, scrutinizing the photo as it sat propped up on her bathroom sink, she cut downward from the arm holes until only an inch of the light purple material was holding the shirt together at the bottom. She cut upwards at a slight angle towards the front, creating a V, where the sides of her breasts would be exposed. Sylvie went to refill her glass before oiling her skin so she wouldn't smear lotion all over her kitchen.

Back in her bathroom, she paged through the photos again. The only difference, besides being a model with fake boobs, was the pubic hair. Sylvie had never considered "going bald," and it sent a tingle of excitement through her. Maybe it was time she tried. She wondered if there was a man with a fetish somewhere who would do this for free, much like *Footworshipper* would give her a pedicure. She made another trip to the kitchen to fetch her computer, wondering if she had the nerve to look. *Maybe later.*

Standing in front of her bathroom mirror, Sylvie stripped off her panties and looked at herself, then looked at the *Playboy* centerfold, spread-legged and hairless. *I should try it, at least once*, she thought, then removed her shoes again, too.

Sylvie climbed into the tub with the scissors and started cutting tufts of pubic hair, careful not to get too close to the skin. When she had cut all she could, she sat on the edge of the tub, ran the water warm, and covered herself with shaving cream. She took a long sip of her drink and began with her razor, shaving very slowly for fear of nicking the delicate skin that had never encountered a blade before.

Twenty minutes passed while Sylvie carefully shaved herself, then she ran the shower to rinse both her newly bald private area and the green mask from her face; she was both scared and excited to view the results. Toweling herself dry, she stepped back in front of the mirror and stared. She blushed a bright red and took another long sip of her drink.

Embarrassed by her own naked, now hairless body, Sylvie was once again emboldened by the magazine propped up on the counter. She found bath oil in her cabinet and rubbed it into her skin, taking extra time to care for the parts that had been newly exposed. She laced up her sneakers and pulled on the sliced-up shirt. The only things missing were the gymnast rings.

Sylvie had a set of TRX suspension straps in the back of her closet which was close enough, in her mind, to the rings. As she walked to her bedroom, the cool air sent thrills to her freshly shaved lips and she began to enjoy the sensation.

The straps were five feet long, and when Sylvie attached them to the shower rod she could lean on them, seeing herself in the mirror and recreating the model's centerfold pose. Hoisting one leg onto the sink, Sylvie angled her body to the left, toward the straps, to show her partial right breast through the cut in her shirt. She held the pose, entranced by what she saw in the mirror. Having natural breasts at her age, she smiled with pride at her body thinking she had done well with the upkeep, even if it didn't look as tight as the picture. She wouldn't be going braless, but certainly had nothing to be ashamed of, either in the gym or on the boat. She relaxed more as she looked at herself in the mirror, her eyes roving over every part of her body as if she had never seen herself before. She clung to the straps and flexed, tightening her biceps and glutes, admiring her well-shaped ass from the side. Sylvie slowly swung her leg open to fully recreate the *Playboy* pose and examine her newly-shaved area, letting her full weight rest on the straps. Staring at her kitty, as Sylvie modestly called her girl parts, oiled and glistening in the light, she couldn't move her eyes away. She opened her legs further, eyes transfixed. It had been so long since she actually looked at her private area in a mirror. She was fascinated.

The curtain rod gave a rubbery groan as it ripped off the tiled wall and sent Sylvie flying sideways out the bathroom door.

Sylvie awoke on Saturday morning with a slight headache, partly from too much tequila and partly from banging her head on the floor when the shower rod broke free from the wall. Instead of fixing it when it came loose, she had thrown the straps, curtain and rod into the bathtub, swept the workout clothing from her bed to the floor, and went to sleep. As the coffee dripped and time to leave for the gym approached, Sylvie had to choose an outfit, eat breakfast, and take a shower; she had too much to do to worry about the date.

In the end, Sylvie wore a loose red tank top, tight black yoga pants, and her favorite purple sneakers. Grabbing a towel and water bottle, she ran out her door, and made it to the gym exactly on time. She didn't have to look around long before *AceLover* found her at the front desk.

"Sylvie? I'm Marcus. You look better than your pictures!"

He didn't, but at least he looked exactly like his picture, which Sylvie took as a positive start to the date. He was wearing loose white shorts with small American flags printed all over them, white high top sneakers, black lifting gloves, and a ripped white shirt that looked suspiciously like the one Sylvie had cut up the previous night; it was almost as if he was looking at the same model when he had his scissors out. His biceps were the most well-developed part of his body, but not so big as to be gross and veiny, she thought. Sylvie immediately wanted to run her hands across his chest; she could see the muscles peeking out the sides of his cut-up shirt, and it was not overly hairy, either, just enough. Moving her eyes downward, she saw legs that didn't receive quite as much attention as his upper body; she wondered why so many men never noticed their own legs. Still, they were decent looking.

Marcus had short brown hair, almost a military cut, big brown eyes, full lips, and that horrible square inch of hair on his chin. Almost perfect, but she wasn't looking for her dream man – just a hot date.

"You look pretty good, yourself. What did you have in mind for today? I work out a lot, but mostly outdoors. I haven't been to a gym in ages."

"Today's my upper back and bicep day, and I always end with 15 minutes on the treadmill. Burns more fat if you lift, then run. Plus, gotta do some cardio, even if I hate it."

"Great. Let's get started."

Marcus took care of Sylvie's day pass at the desk, then led her to the free-weight area. The gym was fairly empty for a Saturday morning – the day was so beautiful and sunny most people had probably opted to go to the beach. Five guys occupied that section of the gym, each with headphones, not paying attention to anyone else.

"You don't have to do what I do if you don't want, but I got a pretty good plan and like to stick to it. I usually work out with the boys, so this'll be a nice change." He openly grinned at her. "I think I could watch you all day."

Sylvie blushed, and thought to herself, *Say something sexy! Flirt! Tell him he's hot! Oh my God, just say anything!*

But the moment passed.

"I'll try your plan. I could use some upper back and bicep work." All her reading on how to make conversation was forgotten, and she would never again write a cheat sheet on her arm.

"Excellent. Let's start with front raise. Grab some weights, nothing too heavy, and watch what I do."

Sylvie picked up two 10-pound dumbbells; she grabbed the red ones to match her shirt. Marcus chose metallic 40-pound weights. He held the weights at his sides and raised them straight up to shoulder level in front of his body, with locked arms, alternating right and left.

"Ten times each side for warmup."

Sylvie copied his movements.

"Next is the same, just out to the side."

She watched his muscles flex, and began to think the soul patch wasn't so bad. Sylvie copied him again.

"Military press. This is still warmup." He held his weights to the side at eye level with elbows bent, and pressed them toward the ceiling until his arms were straight above his head. Sylvie started the 10 reps, but her eyes wandered to his ass; although his shorts were loose, she could see the muscle definition and thought it was a great looking ass. She wondered what it would feel like in the palms of her hands.

Together, they did a few more warmup exercises. Marcus caught Sylvie staring at him in the mirror more than once; at first, Sylvie blushed and quickly looked away, pretending she was merely looking around the room, interested in the other men lifting weights nearby. But Sylvie had made up her mind: this was the guy. He might not be ideal, but he was sexy and she was attracted to him. She was ready for the romantic encounter she could write about, that she needed. The next time he caught her staring, she still blushed, but met his eyes in the mirror and smiled; a smile conveying the promise of much more to come, she hoped.

"Are you ready to start our workout?"

Sylvie was already sweating from the warmup; running and swimming kept her in shape, but lifting weights was a whole different type of workout. She would definitely be sore tomorrow, but wanted to keep up with Marcus.

"Okay, we're doing three sets of eight reps for each of these. Let's start with a standing row."

Marcus selected new, heavier weights, but Sylvie decided to stick with her ten pounds. She watched him bend at his waist and lift the weights to his chest eight times. Even though she knew the proper forms for the sets, Sylvie made up her mind to become *ShySylvie* as best she could, and started her reps with a straight back and elbows bent the wrong way. And just as she thought, Marcus immediately jumped over to correct her form.

He stood behind her and placed his left hand on her left hip, fingers curling to the front of her abdomen; her body tensed at his touch. With his right hand on her upper back, he pushed until she was bent over forty-five degrees.

"With your elbows pointing up and back, pull the weights to your chest."

Sylvie faked being off-balance, causing Marcus to wrap his arms around her waist and pull her tightly back into his body – exactly what she wanted.

"I got you, try it now."

Sylvie did the eight reps, agonizingly slowly, to keep him pressed against her. When she bent over to set down her weights, he kept holding her close, only reluctantly letting her go when she straightened.

"You might try putting one foot out in front of the other for better balance," he said, and walked back to his weights to start another set.

Sylvie progressed through three sets each of bicep curls, reverse flies and hammer curls with Marcus, but there was little reason for him to touch her again until he took her sweaty hand and led her to the far wall of the gym.

"Are you ready for pullups? Last thing before we run."

Sylvie was definitely not looking forward to pullups. She could already feel her arms ache, even using light weights. "I've never been good at these. I'm not sure I can do a single one."

"I'll do a set first, then help you." Marcus jumped to reach the bar and swiftly did ten pullups. Sylvie stood staring at his back muscles, and thought, *this must be the formula for a romantic encounter, doing an activity together that doesn't require making awkward conversation*. She looked straight into his eyes when he let go of the bar.

"I can think of other ways to work on our cardio other than a treadmill," Sylvie softly said, amazed at her daring.

Marcus grinned. "I didn't expect to hear *that*. Wow. But we've got all day, let's finish our workout, and maybe you'll want to come back to my house for a shower after." He didn't look away from her eyes.

"I think I'd like that. And I think I'll skip the pullups and start running. Come find me when you finish here," Sylvie replied as she turned and walked back towards the front of the gym to the row of stationary bikes and treadmills. She wished she had her mobile phone on hand to send a triumphant text to Colleen. With the prospect of finally having a successful romantic encounter, Sylvie hadn't felt so happy in a long time. She practically skipped all the way to the treadmill.

Mirrors covered every wall in the gym, and Sylvie was able to continue watching Marcus do pullups even though she had her back to him. She stood on the sides of the treadmill while pushing the *Quick Start* button, letting the belt slowly start moving before she hopped on; she gradually increased the speed until she was at an easy jog.

She watched Marcus release the pullup bar after his second set and exchange a few words with a nearby lifter. It was obvious now that he knew everyone in the gym, but had ignored them earlier to pay full attention to Sylvie. Maybe he didn't want to take a chance she'd be attracted to one of his friends, she thought, and became increasingly excited about the few minutes of running until they headed back to his place. Her excitement increased exponentially as she increased her running speed on the machine. Sylvie watched Marcus start on his third set of pullups.

> *He dropped to the floor, and walked towards her. She could see the sweat trickling down his neck, and she longed to follow the line with her tongue. As he approached, she reached out and grabbed his shirt; it was wet and torn, and it didn't take any effort to rip it open, revealing his muscular chest. She slowly ran her fingers down his body, starting at the top of his neck, over his throat, one hand lightly brushing each nipple and causing him*

to shiver. Her fingers continued down to his stomach, tracing the outline of his rock-hard abs before moving outward and around to his strong lower back and reaching their destination, his perfectly toned ass. She cupped his cheeks with both hands and pulled him up against her; she could feel his excitement as he pressed against her body. He bent his head to her neck, breathing in her scent, as he gripped the hem of her t-shirt and lifted; she raised her arms in the air and he pulled the shirt over her head, revealing her sweat-soaked, now see-through, bra. He placed his hands on her bottom and lifted; she wrapped her legs around his hips and he walked the few steps to the empty weight bench, setting her down gently. His fingers slid under the band of her sports bra, briefly cupping her breasts as he lifted it over her head, throwing it aside with her shirt. He lowered himself to his knees and ran his tongue upward, between her breasts, her fingers tangled in his hair, guiding his mouth...

"Sylvie!"

Startled awake from her daydream, Sylvie reacted by turning to see who was yelling at her, forgetting she was on a treadmill. Running at seven miles per hour, it took only a fraction of a second to catch the side of her sneaker on the swiftly moving belt. With a shocked scream and desperate hands reaching out to regain balance, Sylvie's legs flew out from under her and she landed face down. The treadmill shot her backward and onto the floor in as ungraceful a way as possible, depositing her at Marcus's feet. When she looked up to tell him she was okay, blood spurted out of her nose, down the front of her shirt, and onto the floor in front of his sneakers.

"And then everyone in the entire place came running to stare at me."

Colleen wrapped her arm around Sylvie as she listened to the story of her gym date. They were sitting alone on Colleen's couch, Mak was putting the children to bed.

"I'm sure it wasn't that bad. You don't look so terrible, I'd hardly notice your black eyes if I wasn't looking for them. They're more like light-brown eyes."

Sylvie took another sip of her red wine. "People were freaking out. I guess they don't see anyone fall off a treadmill very often. Or bleed that much. Marcus was so embarrassed; there weren't many people there but I think they were all his buddies. He offered to take me to the hospital, though."

"Well that was nice of him," Colleen's sarcasm was evident. "If you were getting along so well, why didn't he drive you to his house and take care of you?"

"I'm not sure he was prepared to administer first aid on a first date. Mouth-to-mouth, maybe." She thought for a moment. "It was going so well, too." Sylvie replaced the ice pack on the bridge of her nose and sank back into the couch cushions.

As usual while Sylvie described her dates, Colleen had trouble keeping a straight face. Even though Sylvie had a splitting headache and a swollen nose, Colleen still found the humor of the situation.

"So…any chance for a second date?" she asked with a big smile.

Sylvie drained the remainder of her wine and laid back again. "I think the magic is gone. You should've seen the look on his face. Like he wanted to crawl away and hide. I thought I had sole rights to that look. I've hit my head twice in two days now, I'm not sure I can handle a boat trip tomorrow."

"You hit your head twice?"

"I don't want to talk about it."

"You should still go tomorrow, give this new guy a chance. He's probably so desperate to make new friends he'd do anything, and maybe he really is as cute and sweet as Grace says. And he won't care about your puffy face. Have you spoken to him since you agreed to meet him?"

"No. He sent a text with the details. I meant to ask him to send me a picture but I forgot."

"Send it now so I can see him. I really think you should go. Get it over with. And if it's awful you can change your book to *100 Horrible First Dates*."

"That's not funny."

"Or *What Not Do On A First Date.*"
"Shut up."
"How about *Dating Advice for the Socially Awkward*?"
"I'm going home."

Sunday morning was calm and sunny, a perfect day for a boat trip, but Sylvie was not as excited as she usually was when going on an adventure. Instead of her usual anxiety about first dates, she simply didn't care. She had been on three dates in a short period of time, and none had gone well. All she wanted was a romantic encounter to ignite her imagination for her book, but nothing had gone according to her plans. Her first date was boring, and she felt like an idiot trying to be sexy in her cold, wet bikini while *Surfer1968* made small talk, but no passes. He had given her nothing exciting to write about.

The second date had been even worse; she hadn't even bothered to record the date in her notes, not wanting to remember it at all. She had made a complete ass of herself in front of *Phred69*, smearing ink on her dress and face with her ring tangled in her hair, and wished the evening had never happened. Sylvie was mostly sorry she had to throw out her favorite red dress; she had contemplated various ways to remove the ink stain, but eventually realized she could never wear it again without remembering the disaster that happened when she wore it last.

But the worst by far was her date with *AceLover*, a man she was attracted to, and who was equally attracted to her; she had very publicly and foolishly injured herself while daydreaming on a treadmill, and so recently that the bruises on her face and ego were still visible. Obviously, she hadn't recorded the date in her notebook. She had the photographs Colleen surreptitiously took of her swollen face when her eyes were closed if she really wanted to remember the day.

Sylvie's friendship with Grace was the sole reason she bothered to show up on Sunday morning instead of lying in bed feeling sorry for herself. Even Colleen's early-morning, morale-boosting text *Enjoy your date, it might be amazing!* did nothing to lift her spirits. Sylvie was simply going through the motions as she dressed in a bikini and cover-up, drank coffee, ate a slightly burned bagel, and packed a bag for the ocean trip.

A six-hour trip, trapped on a boat with no way to go home early – this might be the most horrible day ever, Sylvie glumly thought as she drove to the harbor to meet Russ. "Awesome," she said aloud to herself.

When she arrived at 7:15 a.m., dozens of tourists were already loitering around the entry to the boat company's store.

How am I supposed to figure out who my date is? Sylvie idly wondered. She didn't care enough to be worried. She slowly walked to the counter to check in.

"Good morning. My name is Sylvie, and I'm supposed to be meeting Russ Templeton for the boat."

"Good morning, Sylvie," the reservationist replied. "Russ already checked in; he told us to keep an eye out for you. He said it's a blind date – how exciting!"

Before Sylvie could say another word to clarify that it wasn't a blind date as much as it was a favor for a friend, the reservationist walked away from her computer and approached a man standing by the refreshment table. Sylvie watched her tap him on the shoulder and say a few words. They both turned and looked back at Sylvie, a happy smile lighting up the man's face. He picked up two cups of steaming coffee and walked toward her.

Sylvie could tell the man had been living in a place without a lot of sunshine or maybe worked too much to get outside, because the skin of his arms and legs was so white it was almost glowing. He was wearing a light blue t-shirt and blue wave-patterned surf shorts, obviously brand new since she could see the fold creases as if they had just come off the shelf. This was definitely her date – clearly a man who had just moved to the sunny island.

"Hi Sylvie," he said as he handed her a cup of coffee and guided her away from the reservation desk. "I'm so happy that you're coming on this trip with me. I would have felt a little awkward bringing one of the guys from work, plus Grace has told me such wonderful things about you. I'm Russ, as I'm sure you've guessed. And you probably know a lot about me, too, from Grace."

Sylvie didn't, but was happy that Russ kept talking so she wouldn't have to admit it.

"I moved here about three weeks ago, and haven't had much of a chance to take in any sights. I've never been on a boat in the ocean before, so I'm crossing several things off my list: see the coast, go on a boat ride, have a date with a pretty woman, meet new friends. I can't remember the last time I was this excited about a day off."

Sylvie knew she should say something encouraging to him, to share in his excitement of doing new things, but all she could do was put a mildly tolerant expression on her face, sip her coffee, and listen as he continued.

"Six hours of sightseeing on a boat – how lucky are we to be able to do this? I realized this morning that I didn't have anything appropriate to wear; I didn't even own swimming trunks when I moved here. So I came in extra early to buy these clothes and a beach towel. Thank heavens they sell clothes here; otherwise you'd be on a date on a boat with a guy wearing khakis and a button-down. How embarrassing would that be?"

The best Sylvie could manage was a slight sound of amusement, or so she hoped it sounded to him, and let her mind wander away from his nervous chatter. She studied his face as he talked – he really was handsome, just as Grace had said. His hair was blondish-brown, cut short and combed very neatly as Sylvie imagined an engineer would do it – fastidiously precise. His eyes were a stunning bright blue with just a hint of age lines surrounding them, a benefit of having little sun exposure throughout his life. He stood two inches taller than her, and although she guessed he was slightly older, he didn't have the saggy jowls or paunch to suggest he did nothing other than sit at a desk. She wondered what he did to keep in shape, or if it was just genetics. Or maybe he simply didn't drink, which adds so much extra weight as people age.

God, I hope he drinks, she thought, *or this* will *be the longest day ever*.

Sylvie realized Russ was staring at her, as if expecting an answer to a question, but she hadn't been paying attention to what he was saying. Thankfully, she was saved by the boat's captain, calling the guests to gather outside to walk down to the harbor. They turned to follow the crowd of people, conversation momentarily forgotten.

"Aloha and good morning!" the captain cheerfully called to the group. The group, minus Sylvie, replied the same back with equal enthusiasm. "My name is Dylan, and I'll be your captain today. The weather looks great, so follow me down to the boat, where we'll do our safety briefing and get our trip under way."

The mass of people, almost entirely tourists, followed Captain Dylan out of the shop and down to the harbor. Looking around, Sylvie saw dozens of happy people, mostly couples but some with small children, and decided she may as well make the best of the beautiful day. Her headache was nearly gone thanks to the aspirin she took before leaving her house, and the swelling of her nose and darkened eyes were almost unnoticeable. She was on a date with an intelligent, good-looking man, so why not enjoy it? She turned to Russ, put a genuine smile on her face, and said, "I'm glad Grace gave you my number. It's so nice out; I'm excited you'll finally get to see the island from the ocean."

They reached the harbor after a couple minutes of walking and boarded the catamaran; Sylvie guessed the boat was around 60 feet long. The hull was a pleasant deep-blue color, which looked beautiful floating in the clear-blue water. Sylvie had been on these trips at least a dozen times, so she knew the procedure. She led Russ down below to the spacious cabin to store their bags on a window ledge, where they wouldn't get wet, then back to the rear of the boat where Captain Dylan was gathering everyone for the safety briefing.

"I've got a few important safety rules I need everyone to understand before we leave the dock," the captain began. Russ was giving his full attention to the announcements, but Sylvie had heard them enough times to recite it from memory, so she let her mind wander again. She watched the other crew members scurrying around to prepare for departure, guiding a few curious people back to the briefing, making sure ample coffee, pastries and fruit were laid out on the buffet, and finally loosening dock lines. Sylvie's attention was brought back to the captain when everyone around her began to laugh at his joke, then he introduced his crew – Joe, Cory and Alicia – and it was time to leave the harbor.

Taking Russ by the arm, Sylvie led him to the starboard side of the boat, and picked a spot against the thin silver railing.

"The coast will go by on this side; is it okay to stand for a while? I don't feel like squeezing onto a bench, and this'll be the best way for you to see everything."

The ocean was calm enough to comfortably stand without holding on very tight, and together they watched Port Allen disappear in the distance behind them. The terrain turned shades of brown as they motored past the drier side of the island. They passed an abandoned sugar mill and a small beach side town. As Captain Dylan narrated the trip over the loudspeakers with soft Hawaiian music playing in the background, he interrupted his story to shout, "Spinner dolphins up ahead!"

The crowd pressed to the front of the boat as dolphins swam and played in the bow wake. Most people were holding cameras over the sides, exclaiming "Ooh!" and "Aah!" whenever a dolphin jumped out of the water, spun, and splashed back down to continue racing with the boat. Russ and Sylvie leaned over the railing to watch.

"I've never seen dolphins before!" Russ exclaimed, his excitement showing on his face. Sylvie had seen them many times, but they never failed to amaze her, and she felt her heart lighten and her worries fall away. She watched and laughed with the rest of the group until the pod of dolphins swam away from the boat, leaving them to continue the trip up the coast.

"That was incredible! I've never seen anything like it! This could be the best day ever," Russ said as he placed his hand on top of Sylvie's and gave it a gentle squeeze.

Sylvie looked down at his hand, still covering hers, then looked up into his face. "Yes, it *could* be the best day ever," she agreed.

Sylvie and Russ spent an hour marveling at the sights and listening to Captain Dylan narrate the island's history as they motored up the coast along the jagged cliffs. Although the days were generally sunny, fall brought rain to the mountains and the waterfalls were full and flowing. The captain announced the snorkel stop and began to moor the boat while the deckhands walked through the group asking which passengers wanted to get in the water, handing out masks and snorkels. When Cory approached, Russ suddenly looked very intimidated.

"I don't like admitting this, but I never really learned how to swim properly; I was a skier. I didn't think it would be a big deal, but now that I'm out here I'm not sure I have the courage to jump in."

Cory was prepared for this; he handed Russ a plastic, yellow, blow-up life jacket. "It's pretty calm today, so if you want to just get in to cool off, and say you swam in the ocean, we'll show you how to use this. No big deal if you don't want to."

Russ turned to Sylvie, "Will you be embarrassed if I'm swimming with this?"

"Of course not. I think it's great you want to try. I'll stay by you, and we can stick close to the boat; you can get out whenever you'd like. But I definitely think you *should* get in for a few minutes, at least."

Cory gave them two sets of snorkel gear along with the float. "The captain will give another safety briefing and I think you should pay attention to it," he told Russ.

The group gathered at the front of the boat, per the captain's instructions. He pointed out the boundaries of their snorkel area, and asked that the group please stay within them. "Joe and Alicia will be in the water with you if you have any questions or concerns. Cory and I will be watching from the boat." Then he demonstrated the signals to use for a swimmer in distress.

Captain Dylan held up a yellow plastic life jacket. "For those of you who are less confident in the water, I recommend using one of these." He placed it over his head, buckled the thin black straps around his back and between his legs, and blew air into the valve. The float inflated. "Guys, don't pull the bottom strap too tight or your vacation will cease to be romantic." The group laughed.

The captain donned his snorkel mask next, and gave a quick summary of how to breathe through the tube without filling it with water. "Are you ready? Head to the back of the boat, get your fins, and let's get in!"

Russ hesitated for a few moments, looking uncertain, then turned to follow everyone. "I didn't think about this part too much, but I guess I have to do it; then I can add it to my list and cross it off. Go swimming in the middle of nowhere."

Being a confident swimmer all her life, Sylvie had never put much thought into this. Looking at the situation from his point of view, jumping in the water with nothing but mountains and waterfalls in sight, far from any towns or roads – it had to be daunting. She sympathized.

"Just remember that you don't have to stay in long if you don't want to. You don't have to go in *at all* if you don't want to. I'll be with you, and you have a float, so everything will be okay."

They inched forward in line toward the boxes of fins, sorted according to size. "Are there sharks out here?"

Sylvie laughed, and immediately felt bad. "No, not over here. That's why they picked this spot." Russ looked reassured; he was obviously worried enough about swimming and didn't analyze the blatant lie Sylvie had just told him.

They were nearly to the back of the boat, and Russ placed the yellow float over his head. "Don't you want to take off your shirt first?" Sylvie had untied her pareo moments before, and had tied it to the railing.

"No, I'm embarrassed enough with the float, I don't need you to see how pale I am, too." She grabbed the straps and buckled him in while he blew into the inflator valve. Sylvie had a flash of memory as his vest puffed up, remembering the days when she inflated the water wings for Sol and Lily, teaching them how to swim. The memory made her feel a tenderness for Russ that she hadn't expected.

"Before you know it you'll be swimming in the ocean every day, and tan, too."

Reaching the end of the line, they were given fins in their size and sat down at the bottom of the swim steps to put them on. Sylvie was well past ready to get in, but sat with her feet dangling in the water to give Russ a chance to gather his nerves.

"Ready?"

"Whenever you are."

He took hold of her hand, and together they gently lowered themselves into the water. The float stopped Russ from going under, but Sylvie let herself become completely immersed, savoring the feeling of cool weightlessness. She stayed under just long enough to let out her breath and watch the bubbles rise to the surface. She didn't let go of his hand.

Kicking with her fins, she pulled him a few feet from the boat and stopped.

"Are you okay?"

"I'm okay." He was gripping her hand tightly. She floated on the surface for a few long moments so he could get used to being in the water.

"Are you ready to snorkel a bit? If we move a little further away we'll find some fish to look at."

"Lead the way – but not too far."

Sylvie slowly kicked further toward the rocky cliff, pulling Russ along with her. She stopped when she spied a dark shape in the water below.

"Russ, I see a turtle below us! Put on your mask, check him out!"

Russ eagerly slid the mask over his eyes and placed the snorkel in his mouth. Using his legs, he kicked until his body was horizontal, face in the water. Together, they watched the turtle glide majestically beneath them through the clear water until it was out of sight. The sandy bottom was visible 30 feet below. Sylvie was relaxed and happy for the first time on a date. Russ, however, was not; she could feel him thrashing around in the water. She released his hand so he could use it to push his face above the surface. Sylvie gracefully surfaced and watched Russ struggle upright. He ripped the mask off his head.

"It's so deep out here," he panted, out of breath. "How can there be a turtle but no sharks? Did you lie to me?"

"Wasn't the turtle beautiful?"

"I think I need to get out. I'm not ready for this. It's so deep. Too deep." Russ began to splash in a panic, which Sylvie realized was his attempt to dogpaddle back to the boat. He was too frantic to make any distance.

"I got you." She took his hand again, and with a few powerful kicks she pulled him back to the boat. She placed his hand on the swim step and slipped under the water to remove his fins. Cory, watching from the deck, took Russ's mask and snorkel and gave him a hand up. Russ, now seated on the step, quickly pulled his feet out of the water as if something other than Sylvie lurked below, waiting to bite him.

"I'm sorry, I'm not ready for this. It's too deep out here. I couldn't stop thinking of drifting away and getting eaten by something." He was still breathing heavily, as if he had just swam for miles.

Cory handed him the freshwater hose. "No worries. Rinse off and get some sun. You need it."

Sylvie stayed in the ocean, holding onto the step below Russ. "You did good. I think that was enough to cross it off your list. I can help you get more comfortable in the water when you're ready to learn."

Russ didn't look like he ever wanted to touch water again. "I'm sorry, Sylvie."

"You don't need to apologize. I'm just happy you got to see a turtle. Do you mind if I swim some more? I think they open the bar after snorkeling, so grab a drink, relax, find a comfy place to sit, and I'll be back in 15 minutes."

"Yeah, go ahead." Seeing Russ get up to walk to the front of the boat, Sylvie pushed off the step, dove under the water, and kicked several yards away before surfacing. She looked around at the bottom, not nearly as deep as Russ imagined, and chose a cluster of coral to visit; with a deep breath and a few strong kicks, she easily swam to the reef 20 feet below. Small clusters of tiny black fish wove in and out of the fingers of pink coral, and Sylvie watched until she had to surface for a breath. She kicked further toward the cliffs and dove again, the water even shallower, engrossed in different fish trying to hide in a different coral head. She repeated this, enraptured by the underwater world, until she surfaced near Alicia, floating on a surfboard.

"It's about time to get moving again. Would you start making your way toward the boat? We've got a lot of miles to cover, and I'm sure you're ready for lunch."

Several slow swimmers were still behind her, so Sylvie happily swam back to the boat, taking her time to enjoy the scenery in the clear blue water. She emerged at the swim step, took off her fins, mask and snorkel, and placed them on the boat deck. Lifting herself out, she took the freshwater hose and rinsed her hair and face, then walked toward the front of the boat to find her cover-up. Her spirits were high, and she was excited to continue her date with Russ after the refreshing ocean swim.

She found her pareo, but didn't see him seated around the deck. Wrapping the cover-up around her and tying the ends, she walked around the catamaran, hoping to find him at the bar down below. He wasn't there, but Cory was, and she asked for a glass of red wine.

"Have you seen Russ? I just got back onboard and I don't see him anywhere."

"I gave him a beer about 10 minutes ago, but I haven't seen him since. He's not up top?"

"No, I looked everywhere."

Cory skipped out from behind the bar and lowered himself down the ladder leading to the men's restroom. Sylvie could see him knocking, then listening at the door. Several moments later she saw the door swing open, and an even paler Russ leaning on Cory to climb up the stairs.

"Oh God, Sylvie, I'm so sorry," was all Russ could manage, belching, before Cory led him past her, up to the deck of the boat. She grabbed her glass of wine and followed them. Cory sat him down on a bench at the back of the boat.

"The bathroom is the worst place to be if you're feeling sick. Sit out here, get some sun and air, and I'll be back with water and crackers." Cory left him on the bench with Sylvie.

With all the passengers on board again, Sylvie watched the crew scurry around to depart for the remainder of the trip up the coast, her favorite part. Away from all signs of civilization, and watching the grandeur of the mountains float by, she felt a kinship to the scenery, having hiked and camped all along the treacherous coast by herself. Her attention to the scenery was interrupted by a loud belch from Russ as he leaned over the back railing to vomit. He was even whiter than when she had met him, if that was possible. Sylvie sipped her wine.

Cory returned with a glass of ice water and a packet of salted crackers. He handed them to Sylvie. "Better up here than down there," he said, referring to the bathroom. "Lunch will be served downstairs in a few minutes if either of you are up for it." The boat motored up the coast.

Sylvie was ravished after her swim, and had been looking forward to a cheeseburger from the grill. She wasn't sure if she could eat one in front of Russ, which made her feel a little guilty. She had never been seasick, and the sight of him throwing up barely bothered her. She definitely needed lunch.

He sat back against the cushioned seat along the rear of the boat, eyes closed and gasping for breath. "I'm so sorry, Sylvie. I had no idea I would be sick. I got back onboard to wait for you, got a beer and sat down, and all of a sudden thought I was gonna die. The rocking back and forth, I can't do it. Can we go back now?"

Sylvie handed him the ice water. "You need to stay hydrated. We'll be back soon. Drink."

Russ took a sip of water, looked at Sylvie for a short moment, and raced to the rail to vomit it up over the back of the boat. She took another drink of her wine and leaned back into the cushions, putting her feet up. She truly pitied him for feeling so sick, but was not surprised the date had turned bad and returned to her former state of indifference.

"Awesome," she said aloud, knowing he wouldn't hear.

Sylvie eventually made her way to the lunch buffet, after being certain that Russ was as comfortable as possible. He had vomited multiple times, finally dry heaving, until he was able to lay back on the cushioned bench and close his eyes. She pitied him, but she was hungry. She went below and made a plate with a cheeseburger, coleslaw and pineapple chunks, and sat at the bar to eat, where she wouldn't see Russ getting sick, and the food wouldn't make him sicker. She asked for another glass of wine.

Finishing her meal, and being grateful once again because she had never experienced seasickness herself, Sylvie procured a hand towel, filled it with ice, and headed back to the deck to check on Russ. She found him exactly as she left him. He opened his eyes as she sat down.

"I never thought I could feel so awful. I'm sorry, I feel like I've completely ruined your day. Do you know how long until we get back to the dock?"

Sylvie arranged the towel with ice on his forehead, and tried to coax him into taking a sip of water, which he refused. He didn't want to vomit again.

"You haven't ruined my day, don't feel bad about it. If I hadn't come with you, I'd be at home cleaning and doing laundry. I'd much rather be on a boat. It's so beautiful out here; I don't get out here enough." She hoped to distract him from how badly he was feeling by teaching him about the island. "Did you know that you can't get here by car? You can drive to the furthest beach on the west side, Polihale, which is about 17 miles long; then there are another 17 miles of coast with no roads. At the north end, the road ends at Ke'e, another beach. People start there and spend the day kayaking and sightseeing until they end up back on the west side. Maybe someday after you've gotten used to the water you can try that. There are all sorts of sea caves and waterfalls to visit when you're on a small boat, and tiny beaches to paddle up to where you sit and eat lunch." She thought about his situation for a moment and added, "If you're paddling your own kayak you probably wouldn't get sick."

Russ pushed himself further up the bench, placing his head in Sylvie's lap, and closed his eyes again. *Crap*, she thought, *I should've gotten another glass of wine before I sat down.* She was stuck.

She only had to wait a few minutes, however, until Cory came back to check on them. Russ didn't open his eyes when Cory asked how he was feeling, so Sylvie assumed he had fallen asleep.

"Would it be possible to get another glass of red wine? I can't get to the bar right now."

Cory was back quickly after reassuring her he'd check on her often, and bring the wine bottle for refills. Sylvie put her feet up on the back railing. At some point during lunch, she hadn't noticed exactly when as she was down below, the crew had raised the boat's sails and cut the motors; they had reached the half-way point of the six-hour trip and turned back toward home. Quietly sailing, with only the sound of the water, and soft Hawaiian music coming through the speakers, Sylvie leaned her head back on the cushions, completely at ease, and closed her eyes …

> *She noticed him watching her from across the boat. She was lying alone on a long, cushioned bench at the back, away from the large group of people. She had untied her cover-up, and was sunbathing in only her bikini. The scant, white fabric contrasted breathtakingly with her browned and gleaming skin, and in a moment of shyness, she reached for the pareo to cover herself from his hungry eyes. His stare made her feel naked.*
>
> *"Please, don't," he said softly as he approached. "It would be a shame to conceal such beauty."*
>
> *She looked up, and fully noticed him for the first time. He was tall and lean, each muscle perfectly defined as his long strides brought him closer. His untamed, curly brown hair was sun-kissed with streaks of blonde. He reached the bench where she lay, and knelt down next to her, taking her bottle of sunscreen in his hands.*
>
> *"I don't want to see your gorgeous skin get burnt. You look like you need more lotion, and I can reach all the places you might have missed. Turn over, and let me start with your back."*
>
> *She agreed, rolled onto her stomach, and settled herself into the cushions. She closed her eyes and heard*

the snap of the bottle opening. He squirted a generous amount of the cream into his hands and rubbed them together to warm the lotion before placing his hands on her lower back. Her body stiffened at his touch, making her jump.

"Relax, let me take care of you."

Again, she closed her eyes. She reveled in the sensations his hands produced in her body as he slowly caressed her skin. Moving upward, she felt him tug the strings and release her bikini top. He added more lotion to his hands and smoothed it across the top of her back and neck, lightly grazing the sides of her breasts. She gasped at the unexpected pleasure, wanting more, but he did not touch her there again.

He ran his hands along her upper arms where they lay on either side of her head, then, lightly skimming her skin with his fingertips, she felt him move all the way down to her legs. Adding more lotion to his hands, he started at her ankles, then rubbed her calves, and worked his way to the backs of her thighs, each hand making identical movements on her legs. She realized she was holding her breath in delicious anticipation of where his fingers might touch next.

After reaching the bottom of her skimpy bikini, he let his fingers barely penetrate the boundary of the fabric; she felt his thumbs move to her inner thighs, gliding upward, until they, too, reached the material. Adding slightly more pressure, his thumbs moved in miniscule increments up her bikini line, causing a pleasurable aching feeling deep inside her belly. She shuddered again, under his hands, as his thumbs completed the trip up her bikini line. She wanted more, but he removed his hands from her.

She heard the squirt of more lotion. "You have such soft skin. Let me make sure the front of your body is protected, too."

Opening her eyes, she looked around but could not see any other people from the low bench where she lay. Turning to her side, she felt the small triangles of her untied bikini top slide against her nipples, completely exposing her full breasts. Feeling shy again under his gaze, she reached for the white material as she wriggled onto her back. He gently grabbed her wrists, and she allowed him to place her hands above her head and completely remove her top.

With almost painfully slow movements, he rubbed the lotion in circles on her breasts, careful not to touch her nipples. She thought her body would catch fire with the heat generated from deep inside. She squirmed on the bench, unable to keep still any longer. She had to have him, and a glance at his shorts told her he was ready as well. She sat up on the bench, causing him to lean back, but not far enough to escape her grip. One of her hands found his hair, she grabbed a handful and guided his face towards her, while the other touched his stomach and slowly continued downward to ...

"Sylvie!"

Caught dreaming, and shocked back into reality, Sylvie jumped. Her full glass of wine jumped with her and spilled down her front, drenching both herself and the top of Russ's head, who had been staring up at her from his prone position. The wine trickled into his eyes, and he scurried to get up.

Already nauseous, the smell of wine added to the sudden movement of jumping off the bench and caused Russ to begin heaving again; he barely made it to the back of the boat. It didn't matter, though, because there was nothing left in his stomach to come up. He remained at the rail for a few minutes while Sylvie mopped up the wine from the bench with her pareo.

She got up to help Russ when Cory returned to check on them, a glass of ice water in one hand and a bottle of wine in the other. He grinned as he took in the scene.

"What's going on, guys?"

Russ did not look happy, and Sylvie did not blame him. He was having a bad enough day without red wine running down his face, staining his shirt. Cory set down the glass of water and pulled the freshwater hose from the hook nearby.

"Rinse off, it'll probably make you feel better." He turned to Sylvie. "More wine?"

"Yes, please," she whispered, holding out her empty glass.

She rinsed out her cover-up when Russ finished with the hose, and together they sat in silence for the next hour until the boat docked at the harbor. Sylvie couldn't think of anything to say as they walked up to the parking lot.

As they reached his car, she said, "Sorry you had a bad day. And sorry about the wine, too. Can I buy you a new shirt?"

"Don't worry about it, just an accident. I need to get myself into a shower and bed. I'll see you later." He turned to get into his car.

"I hope you feel better…"

Russ pulled away, leaving Sylvie standing alone in the lot.

When Sylvie arrived home, she dumped her bag out on the kitchen floor, searching for her phone. She had kept it sealed in the bag all day to protect it from the salt water, and was eager to check her messages. After another bad date, she was still hopeful Michael would call, somehow certain everything would be different with him. Perhaps she was hopeful because she couldn't bear going on another blind date, and she felt she knew what to expect from him.

She dreaded logging onto the dating site again, believing that every encounter was doomed to end in humiliation.

She found her phone and switched it on, finding four new text messages, but no unknown numbers.

Three of the texts were from Colleen, impatiently asking about the boat trip. The fourth was from Grace, *I can't wait to hear about you and Russ! You're perfect together, right??* Smiley face, smiley face, smiley face.

Sylvie tossed her phone back onto the pile of items with her bag on the floor, stripped out of her wet, stained pareo and bikini, and headed for the shower for a long, hot scrub.

That evening as Sylvie contemplated the week ahead, and life in general, she came to a decision. Using the dating site to gain romantic experience for her book was not working, and she saw no point in continuing. She hadn't called or returned Colleen's texts, but she could hear Colleen's voice in her head, *Keep trying! You've barely met any men; sooner or later you're bound to find someone who clicks with you. Plus, and I think you can agree with me on this, you've already experienced the worst that can happen on a date. It can't possibly get worse.* Even as an imagined, disembodied voice, she heard Colleen poking fun at her. Sylvie's self-esteem was at an all-time low.

She reached into the very back of the highest shelf in her kitchen pantry, where she kept her I'm-having-a-really-bad-day comfort food. Surprised that she hadn't depleted the stash in the past few weeks, she found an unopened bag of oil-fried, salted, crinkle-cut potato chips. The perfect dinner for her mood.

Ripping the bag open as she sat down at her kitchen table, Sylvie stuffed three giant chips into her mouth and reached for her computer; she planned on deleting her online dating account. She logged on and found 18 new messages and three replies. She decided to read the replies before deleting her profile, out of curiosity.

The first reply was from *Surfer1968*, dated several days earlier; she remembered deleting his last message without replying. Hi Sylvie, I never heard back from you. Maybe you didn't get my message, I don't know how reliable this site is. Anyway, I'd still like to take you out to dinner. Please get back to me with a reply, or even better, call me. He left his phone number for the second time.

Sylvie stuffed more chips into her mouth. "You were boring, can't imagine the next date being any more exciting," she mumbled to her computer screen, spraying it with small bits of chewed chips. *Delete.*

The second reply was from *AceLover*. She stared at the notification, wondering if it would be better for her ego if she just deleted it unread. She gathered the shreds of her courage, ate a couple more potato chips, and clicked on the message. I hope your feeling better. Kinda freaked me out, never seen someone get hurt like that. I'd be totally into it if you wanted to work out with me again. We can skip the running.

Sylvie thought for a moment, grabbed another handful of chips while contemplating the pros and cons of a follow-up date, and forgetting that she had logged on only to delete her account. *He was hot* came to mind first. *He thought I was hot* was a quick second. She ate more chips as she thought. *He could have salvaged the day taking care of me, but instead he ran away.*

"Big baby, afraid of a little blood," she said aloud, with a few more bits of moist chip flying. *Delete.*

The third reply was from *Footworshipper*, although she had never written back to him after his initial message. ShySylvie, I hope you understood that I was serious. That was all of the message, but Sylvie had lost that glimmer of mischievousness that would have allowed her to respond. *Delete.*

Again, instead of deleting the entire account, she looked at the 18 new emails. Her curiosity was temporarily piqued, but the moment she saw the screen name *GotSumtin4U*, she deleted them all. *No more idiots, I'm done*, she thought. *But I probably should let Goodlife_49 know that I'm cancelling our date.* She reached for more potato chips as she scrolled through past messages to find him.

> Aloha, Goodlife. I'm sorry to have to break our date, but I'm unable to meet you next week. I hope you have a wonderful trip and enjoy the island.

Sylvie closed her computer, forgetting to delete her dating profile. She was lost in thought as she shoveled more chips into her mouth.

The day had turned to darkness as she sat quietly in her kitchen, yet she didn't get up to turn on a light. Her thoughts turned to the book she longed to write, and the failure that had dogged her since the beginning. Maybe she was destined to be an accountant for the rest of her life, getting a few weeks off each year to see the world and putting money in her retirement account in order to provide comfort in her old age. Maybe she would spend her years alone, never finding a partner, never learning what true romance actually was.

"Fuck that," she said aloud, letting her true, positive nature shine through the gloom in her mind, and adding more bits of mangled chip to her kitchen table.

When Sylvie awoke on Monday morning, she felt more determined than she had in a long time. Deep down, she felt she was meant for more in life than an ordinary existence. Thinking back on her dates as she showered for work, she realized she had some very positive experiences in the midst of all the negatives. Why not turn those into her book? She set her mind to begin writing after work.

But getting through work was a whole different matter. Grace was convinced she had set Sylvie up with the perfect man for her, so she had told everyone in the office about Sylvie's blind date the previous day. And since everyone knew, again through Grace, about the envelope stuffed with condoms, Sylvie walked into an office of cheering, supportive coworkers. The fact she wasn't scowling seemed to mean everything had gone perfectly. Sylvie wished she had texted Grace back the previous evening, if only to stop the half-dozen people from wondering how soon she'd be married.

After Sylvie had stashed her lunch in the break room refrigerator and sorted through the weekend mail, she called Grace up to her office, ignoring the pink post-it note with Grace's curly handwriting stuck to her monitor, *Come tell me everything!* She didn't want any passers-by to hear the conversation. Grace practically flew up the stairs, and stared at Sylvie with a giant grin and wide, expectant eyes.

"It sucked, and I doubt he'll ever want to speak to me again."

Sylvie could see Grace physically deflate, like a punctured ball.

"I tried, and I really liked him, but I'm just not good at dating. I really appreciate that you tried, though. Thank you."

Grace simply stared back at Sylvie, her wide eyes showing a hint of moisture. After a few moments, "Would you want to try again? What happened? Maybe it was just a bad day. I was so sure you'd hit it off."

"It was a bad day, and I made it worse. I don't think he'd want to go out with me again. Can you tell everyone who thinks I found my true love? I can't bear to explain it to so many people."

Grace stepped forward and grabbed Sylvie in a hug. "We'll find someone for you," she said with the seriousness of a doctor talking to a patient waiting for a new liver. She turned and walked out of the office.

Grace was quick to spread the news to the rest of the office; the people who had wished her well earlier in the day were suddenly too busy working to look up when Sylvie walked by, which was fine with her. She concentrated on the day's work and went straight home, determined to begin writing her book.

Sylvie cleared everything off her kitchen table except her computer, her notebook and pen, a bottle of tequila, and a glass. While waiting for the computer to start, she filled her glass with ice and poured a generous drink. She opened the notebook and found the only entry from her beach date with *Surfer1968*. She ripped it out, crumpled it into a ball, and tossed it on the kitchen floor. "Useless," she grumbled at it.

She held her pen poised above a blank page, ready to write. "Let's make a list of things I know," she told her pen. "I need a man and a woman, so let's figure out who they are. What did I like the best about the men I met?" Sylvie sipped her drink to head off any unwanted feelings of inadequacy from her dating experiences.

"*Surfer1968*: He wasn't super-hot. But I liked the sunset at the beach; we could have a sex scene on a beach blanket, with the sky exploding in beautiful colors behind us." She turned to another blank page and wrote *Scenery*, and added the information.

"*Phred*: Ugh, no. But maybe we should have a really hot hiking scene," she tried to visualize it in her mind. "I've had sex during a hike at the top of a waterfall, and it was the most unsexy thing I've probably ever done in my life; all sweaty and dirty, but not in the good way. Maybe my couple can meet while they're hiking the same trail." She added the new information to the *Scenery* page.

"*AceLover*: Pretty sexy date, up until the end. But if my couple meets on a hiking trail, are they really going to go to the gym together? I doubt it, I think they're going to be outdoor people. He was pretty hot, though." Sylvie turned back to the first blank page in the notebook, and wrote *Man*. "This is why women read romance novels, for the dream man. What did I like best about him?" Sylvie sipped her drink as she called up a mental picture of Marcus, and began to add items to the list, concentrating on his muscular attributes. "Not that stupid patch of hair on his chin, though."

She poured another drink.

"Russ: Beautiful blue eyes." She added it to the list. "Or should my guy have brown eyes?" She wrote *Maybe* after the eye color. She hadn't thought specifically of what her main male character would look like, apart from *tall* and *handsome*. "There should definitely be a boat scene, but without all the barfing. It'll have to be a private boat. A small sail boat. Maybe my guy is a boat captain she meets on a hiking trail. Or he owns a yacht, and they can have champagne and sex in the hot tub while the captain and crew sail them around to exotic ports."

She sipped her drink and thought for a moment. *I don't know anything about people who own yachts; small sailboat, it is.* She added a brief description of the catamaran trip with Russ to the *Scenery* page.

"But Russ was intelligent, and my guy should definitely be smart. No one wants to read about a sexy idiot, unless he doesn't say a word. Or is ridiculously sexy," Sylvie said to her waiting notebook. She thought some more. "No, he should be smart. And charming. Too bad I didn't meet any charming men to write about." She added *smart* and *charming* to the list for her man.

"Well, it's not a great list for my guy, but it's a start. A sexy, charming, smart, muscular, tall, boat-owning, possibly blue-eyed man who likes to hike." She got up to add more ice to the tequila in her glass, then sat back down to go over her list again. "Maybe I should start hanging out at the harbor to see if he exists in real life." Sylvie threw down her pen, somewhat frustrated by her lack of imagination.

She was interrupted from further thought about the man when her phone rang. It was Colleen, whom she still hadn't called back; she was not looking forward to telling her about the date with Russ. *Might as well get it over with*, she thought, and spent the next hour listening to Colleen's laughter. Finally, though, Sylvie was able to laugh with her.

Sylvie brought her notebook to work the next day in case she had any sudden inspiration about her main male character. She hadn't gotten back to the project after speaking with Colleen the previous evening; she had thoroughly enjoyed Sylvie's description of the boat date. Colleen reiterated her idea of writing a comedy about dates gone wrong instead of a romance novel.

Sylvie got through her morning paperwork rather quickly, and her mind wandered back to her writing. She picked up her notebook and began to leisurely walk through the offices, looking at each of the men with whom she worked. She realized she hadn't thought about using any of them in the book.

The first office next to hers belonged to another accountant, a 30-something, African-American man named Byron. She poked her head in.

"Hi. Are you busy?"

"A bit, but come on in. What can I do for you?"

Sylvie took a seat in front of his desk.

Byron was one of her well-wishers after her failed date with Russ. Although he was married, he and Grace had a close relationship, and Sylvie had heard Grace's husband refer to him as her "office husband." He was a very good-looking man.

"Just checking in, seeing how everything's going. I have a pretty light day and can pick up some extra work if you're overloaded." She didn't actually want to, but hadn't thought up any other reason to stop by his office.

"I've got the usual stuff; it would probably take more time to explain this client to you than to just do it myself," he said. "How have you been? Grace was pretty excited about the date she set you up with, I hope you don't mind me asking about it."

Sylvie blushed. "Just a bad day; nothing too horrible. Life goes on." She hoped meaningless platitudes would keep him from asking too many questions.

"My wife is pretty active socially. I bet she knows some quality guys who would be interested in someone like you. You're quite a catch, and I know you're smarter than all of us put together." He grinned. "Should I ask her?"

"Oh God, no," Sylvie scrambled up from the chair, as if she couldn't get away fast enough, almost knocking a picture of Byron and his wife off the cubicle wall. "I just stopped in to say hi, nothing more. I need some recovery time from my last bad date before I go on another one. Thanks for the thought, though."

She walked out of his office, but didn't get much further than a few feet away; she opened her notebook to the *Man* page. "Maybe he has dark skin," she thought, and quickly jotted down Byron's description before she could get caught in the hallway stealing glances back in his office door.

Sylvie walked through the rest of the offices but didn't find anyone else of interest. Her boss was too old, and quite rotund, but could almost be called charming – almost. She didn't think anyone became a CPA if they were too charming. Another coworker, Derek, was good looking and tall, but completely bald. A romance novel had too many possible opportunities for wind blowing through his hair– or hair pulling, or dripping hair as he emerged from the ocean – to use a bald man. He did have an exceptionally nice nose, though. She took note of it in her notebook and headed back to her desk.

Sylvie had to go to the bank that afternoon, and loaded the notebook in her bag in case she saw someone who met her vague description of the hot blue-eyed sailor, or gave her new ideas. She secretly hoped she would run into Michael, the dreamy construction worker, but was also afraid to see him. If Crystal, the bank teller, had given him her business card and he simply wasn't interested, she thought it would be too embarrassing to even look at him again.

She bolstered her confidence and pushed open the front door of the bank. It was a small lobby, and a quick look around assured her that he wasn't in line. Sylvie didn't recognize anyone else, so she quietly waited for her turn.

After just a few short minutes she walked up to an open teller window. "Sylvie, haven't seen you in a while! How are you, honey?"

"Oh, pretty good, nothing much changes. I haven't been here lately, how's everything with you?"

Before she could answer, the teller in the next window poked her head over the divider, after telling her customer she'd be right back. It was Crystal. "Sylvie! I still have your business card! Maybe he lost his job, or got transferred to a job up north, I don't know. Haven't seen him lately, just wanted to let you know." Sylvie felt a small rush of happiness that she hadn't been rejected.

The first teller looked curious. "Who?"

"That delicious construction boy we always drool over. I thought he'd be good for Sylvie, since we're both married. Although I'm not sure I could say no if his eye turned my way."

"Oh he is so hot! I know exactly who you mean. I would trade my first-born for a night with him."

"Your first-born is 26 years old! You can't trade him anymore."

"If he's still living in my house, I can trade him. Take all three, my husband wouldn't even notice till football season is over. Maybe not even then."

The elderly woman at the second window, having been deserted in the middle of her transaction, shuffled over next to Sylvie. Instead of impatience and anger, she wanted to know which man they were discussing. Life in a small town had its peculiarities.

"You might think I'm nearly dead, but I'd at least like to see this boy you'd wreck your marriages for."

The first teller answered her. "Sorry, Mary. He's a Thursday guy, and you're a Tuesday. Try switching days next week; you'll see who we're talking about if he comes back."

"I'm on a schedule. I'll see what I can do. I see the great-grandkids on Thursdays. And speaking of schedules, can I finish up? I have to get to the grocery store before dark." She winked at Sylvie.

Sylvie returned home after a boring yet unexpectedly busy afternoon at work. She ate a quick dinner before clearing off her kitchen table to sketch out more ideas for her novel. "Maybe I should concentrate on the woman," she told her pen. She didn't bother to boot up her computer this time.

She opened to another blank page and wrote *Woman* at the top. And stared at it. For a long time.

"Should she be based on a real woman I know, or made up to sound perfect?" she asked her pen. "I think women readers would appreciate someone who is just like them. Colleen's well-above average, but not perfect; maybe she should be my female lead."

Although Sylvie could easily recall an image of Colleen in her head, she went to her living room to retrieve her phone to look through recent photos from the beach. It was on the coffee table, and as Sylvie bent to pick it up, she spied the *Penthouse* magazine peeking out from under a small stack of unopened mail. She recalled thinking the cover model should be her main female character, and opened the magazine to the centerfold. "Gigi," she remembered aloud. "And your hairless girl parts don't intimidate me anymore! Mine are like that, too," she told the picture. "But starting to get stubbly."

Paging through the center of the magazine, and still amazed at what some people can do in front of a camera, Sylvie went back to the kitchen table. "Do I want a supermodel-type woman or a regular woman?" She dialed Colleen's number on her phone.

"Hey Sylvie, how's your face?"

"It's completely better, thanks for asking. You got a minute to talk?"

"Sure, whatcha need?"

"If you were to read a romance novel, which would…"

"If I had a moment to read, it wouldn't be a romance novel," Colleen interrupted.

"Okay, but suppose you were going to read one. Would you…"

"I wouldn't. I just said that."

"Okay, but you're going to read *my* romance novel, right?"

"Only if it includes barfing and diving headfirst off treadmills."

Sylvie huffed with impatience. She knew the only way to get Colleen to listen was to let her get her jokes out of the way first.

"Okay, say you're going to read my book that has some romance but includes barfing and face planting and lots of embarrassing moments."

"I might be interested. Go on."

"Would you rather read about a perfect, super-model-type woman or someone normal?"

"What's your favorite designer label?" Colleen asked.

"Uh, I don't know, I buy my work clothes from Macy's. On sale." Sylvie wondered why Colleen was changing the subject.

"How about your favorite shoes? Who makes them?"

"OluKai."

"Those are your flip flops. They're nice, but they're still flip flops. Tell me this – what label are the heels I left at your house?"

Sylvie had never noticed. She was silent while she tried to search her memory, but couldn't come up with anything.

"Let's make it very simple. Can you name a single high-fashion brand name?"

Sylvie thought for a moment. She regularly bought clothes from Athleta, stylish and trendy workout wear, but knew that wasn't the answer Colleen was looking for. "Can you just answer my question?"

"I already answered it. The shoes are $400 Louboutins, by the way, so I hope you've treated them better than you treat your mother. If you didn't recognize that name, and you can't come up with any clothing designers, how are you going to write about a supermodel? You barely know how to apply lip gloss. I think you need to stick with some sort of beach romance. Maybe your girl is pretty, but stick with what you know."

"So no fake boobs, then?" Sylvie asked sarcastically.

"Sure, give her fake tits if you want, they're cheap so everyone's got them now. And really, I'd love it if you wrote about a super model barfing and nose-diving – there's great humor to be found there. But you don't know anything about that world. Write about someone like yourself; I think that would work best for you."

"Okay, I get it. Regular girl."

"How's the book coming along? Much progress lately?"

"Not a lot. I think I've definitely pinned down the size and shape of the man's nose, and that he has long-ish hair. Maybe I just need some time to get past my less-than-romantic dates before I can really get to work. I'm a little frustrated."

"What you need is to get laid. Fuck romance. Call the guy from the gym, you were so close to getting some. Just do it, and I think you'll get some different perspective. And get those bad dates off your mind."

"I can't call him. It was too embarrassing. And I lost any respect I might have had for him, which wasn't much to begin with. How am I supposed to sleep with a guy I know doesn't care anything about me?"

"Wow, you have a lot to learn about one night stands. That's sort of the point of them, to sleep with someone you don't really care about. Who cares what he thinks?"

Colleen and Sylvie both spent a moment thinking in silence.

Very gently, Colleen said, "I get it now. It's not about the book anymore. Sure, you still want to write another book, but after looking for someone online and going on dates, you realize what's missing from your own life, but you don't want to admit it. If this was still just research, you wouldn't have any problem sleeping with him. You don't want to find the steamy sex scene; you want to connect with someone and let him into your heart."

"Shut up, I do not," Sylvie said weakly. But neither of them believed her.

Sylvie lay awake in bed most of the night, wondering if Colleen's accusation had any merit. Was that why she couldn't write about romance, even if it was just some dream-like sex scenes? Was it because she hadn't felt any passion in her own heart for so long?

She thought back to the last time she thought she was in love. He was a little older than her, but not much. He regularly told her he loved her, yet could never find the time to see her; he was married to his job. Each day she would wait for him to return her calls, only to realize he found dozens of more important things he needed to do instead of being with her. It took her months to finally let go, to understand that her dream of a perfect life with this man would never happen, regardless of how many promises he made.

The time before that, Sylvie had instantly fallen for a man she met on the beach. It seemed like a mutual love. They moved in together after only a few weeks of dating and began to plan the rest of their lives. At the time, Sylvie couldn't remember ever having been happier, cooking his favorite meals and having someone to take care of. One day, after living together for two years, she took a day off to surprise him at work with an anniversary lunch and caught him getting cozy with a coworker. When Sylvie demanded to know what was going on, his coworker became equally upset – she had been dating him for almost a year. Sylvie moved out of the house that day, and spent the next few months wondering how she could have been so blind as to miss a year-long affair.

Finally, Sylvie fell asleep; it was an unrestful sleep broken by unhappy dreams. When her alarm rang three hours later, she stayed in bed. She called her office, knowing it would still be empty, and left a voicemail saying she wouldn't be coming in to work. She switched off her phone.

Sylvie kept the drapes closed, and lay in the cool darkness of her bedroom, shutting out the world.

The day was creeping toward sunset when Sylvie finally crawled out of bed. She had heard someone knocking on her door a couple hours previously, but ignored it. She realized who it was when she stepped outside to retrieve her mail – a package lay on her doorstep. Her *Victoria's Secret* order had arrived.

Sylvie placed the unopened box on her kitchen table and switched on her phone. She had five new messages. The first was from her mother, wondering if Sylvie would be flying home for the holidays; she'd call her back tomorrow. The next three were work calls, and she guessed it was probably just Grace worrying if Sylvie needed a ride to the hospital. It was too late to worry about them if they were about clients, but she listened anyway. All three were from Grace, which made Sylvie smile, knowing her friend so well. She sent a quick text assuring her she was not in pain or mortal danger, and thanked her for her concern. The fifth message was a number she didn't recognize. She pressed play, and nearly dropped her phone while she listened.

"Hi Sylvie, this is Michael Brooks. I went to the bank today and was given your business card. Normally I wouldn't call someone I don't know, but Crystal, and really everyone who works there, told me I *had* to call you. They made me promise to ask you out on a date. Actually, they threatened to overdraw my checking account and send me to collections if I didn't call. Then set their sons on me. With their dogs. Those women *really* like you. And I know who you are, even though we've never met. So, would you like to go out this weekend? Call me back."

Sylvie listened to the message twice before putting down the phone. She rummaged through her refrigerator and pulled out the ingredients for dinner, then listened to the message again, almost in disbelief. He had really called.

Sylvie didn't have any business at the bank the next day, so she used her lunch break to stop in. She wanted to speak with the tellers before she returned Michael's call. She entered the back of the line, and Sylvie wasn't standing there for five seconds before she was noticed and called forward, ahead of six people in front of her.

"I don't have any transactions, I'll only be a second," she reassured the other patrons as she cut to the front of the line. Sylvie was sensitive to how angry people easily became when waiting in lines, and she didn't want to feel their hateful stares on the back of her head. The other patrons also knew the women who worked at this particular bank branch and were no longer surprised at anything they did.

All business stopped when Sylvie approached the teller line. Both tellers called some variation of "Be right back" to their clients and ran to the closed window to speak with Sylvie.

"Sylvie, Sylvie, our hottie came back yesterday! I was ready with your card, and I convinced him you'd make a good couple. I'm sure he's gonna call you," Crystal bubbled at Sylvie.

"He didn't say anything about why he's been away from us for so long, but since he agreed to call you, I doubt he's gotten another girlfriend yet," the second teller, Annie, said. Although if I looked like him I'd have at least seven, one for each day of the week so I wouldn't get bored."

Crystal stuck up for Sylvie. "He wouldn't need more than one girlfriend if she was our Sylvie! She's way more woman than any man I know can handle." She glared at the second teller, silently reprimanding her for her disloyalty.

She turned back to address Sylvie directly. "I know he's gonna call you, honey. He had that sparkle in his eye when I described you. He knew immediately who you were, so I'm pretty sure he was already sweet on you."

Sylvie took advantage of the short break in conversation. "Did he look excited, or did he just say he'd call to make you stop talking? You really don't know where he's been?" She lowered her voice, "No strange checks being cashed as a clue?" She didn't want to let on that he had already called her.

"No, no clues. And he's not much of a chatterbox so we didn't get anything out of him. You'll have to fill us in when you go out."

The sound of a throat clearing and keys jingling against the counter reminded the tellers they had jobs to do; they could deal with angry customers if they had to, but knew when they were pushing their luck. They slowly walked back to their stations as Sylvie headed for the exit, with an apologetic smile for everyone she passed.

"Come in the moment you hear from him!"

"We want pictures!"

"Sexy ones!"

The intelligence Sylvie had gathered at the bank was not worth as much as she had originally hoped, although she wasn't sure exactly what she had been looking for to begin with. She debated calling Colleen for advice, but instead, decided it was just time to call Michael and get the initial awkward greeting over with.

Sylvie was sitting at her kitchen table staring at her phone. She replayed Michael's message, then put her phone back on the table. She got up and poured a glass of red wine; she took a couple sips before reaching for her phone and playing the message yet again, enjoying the deep baritone of his voice.

Just fucking do it, she told herself. Her heart was pounding as she dialed his number. It rang five times before going to voicemail, "This is Michael, leave a message." Sylvie was already in love with the sound of his voice.

The tone sounded to begin her message and Sylvie's mind went blank; she hadn't considered what she would say to a recording. With shaking hands, she impulsively hung up and threw her phone on the table.

Idiot, she berated herself. *He'll see I called. What is my problem? How hard is it to leave a stupid message?*

And just as the beginnings of tears stung her eyes, the phone rang.

"Hello?"

"Hi, Sylvie? Did you just call me? This is Michael."

"Oh, yes I did. I was just about to leave you a message when I dropped my phone." *Oh great*, she thought. *First thing out of my mouth is a lie.* "How are you?"

"I'm good, thanks. Like I said in my message, the women at the bank were pretty insistent that I call you; they're certain we'll hit it off. So, would you like to go out with me on Saturday evening?"

Sylvie paused for the smallest moment; she was afraid to appear too eager, but didn't want him to think she was hesitant about going out with him. "Yes, I would love to. Do you have anything in mind? Should we meet somewhere?"

"I do have something in mind, but since I'm asking you out, I'm going to pick you up and drive you home. Why don't I come get you at 6 o'clock on Saturday? Is that okay?"

"It's perfect." Sylvie had no second thoughts about giving Michael her address, as opposed to the other men she had gone out with; his calm, confident manner put her at ease. She told him where she lived. "What should I prepare for?"

"Let's start off with dinner and see how it goes. I'll see you Saturday."

"Great, I can't wait. Thanks for calling."

Sylvie twirled around her kitchen, her phone standing in for a dance partner. She was the happiest she'd been in several days. She had a date, and was not feeling the least bit of anxiety about it. She sent a quick text to Colleen with a brief message, and too many smiley faces. Then she walked to her bedroom and peered into the closet. "What am I going to wear?" she asked her clothes.

The following week, Colleen left yet another message on Sylvie's voicemail, the seventh in almost as many days, but now more anxious than the previous ones; the messages started out jokingly about another embarrassingly bad date, then angry at being ignored, and finally worried. They had all gone straight to voicemail. She didn't understand why Sylvie had not reported back to her about the date with the hot construction worker, or heard from her at all. Sylvie always checked in with her, especially after a date, good or bad, and this was one date Sylvie had been especially looking forward to. Sylvie had called to get an approval for her outfit an hour before Michael was scheduled to pick her up on Saturday, having texted pictures of the different dresses as she them tried on. Colleen had clearly heard the excitement in her voice, and didn't understand the lack of communication.

She wasn't worried that Sylvie had been murdered, or was lying in the hospital on life-support with no way to identify herself; Colleen was her emergency contact at work and if she hadn't been showing up, she was sure she would have received a phone call. Grace personally would have tracked down every one of Sylvie's friends and relatives if she was missing, and organized an island-wide search party, scouring the forests with packs of dogs and leaving a trail of *Have You Seen Me?* fliers every five feet, stapled to telephone poles and posted in store windows. Grace could be counted on for that. She was worried that Sylvie had suffered a final, crippling blow to her self-esteem, and had given up on her hopes of both writing and dating, and was immersed in a deep depression. Colleen felt she had no choice left but to use her lunch break to drive to Sylvie's office to confront her in person.

Colleen greeted Grace as she walked past the front desk on her way to Sylvie's office.

"Hi, Grace. I'm just stopping by to see Sylvie." She only made it a few steps past the front desk before Grace stopped her.

"She's not in. Do you have something to drop off? You can leave it with me."

"Is she out for lunch? Any idea when she'll be back?"

Grace knew that Colleen was Sylvie's best friend, so she had a puzzled look on her face. "Sylvie hasn't been in all week, I was hoping you could tell me where she was. She spoke to her boss about taking some time for personal reasons, and sent instructions about her clients. Other than that, I haven't talked to her. All my calls went to voicemail and I don't know where she is."

Colleen turned and ran back out of the building without replying to Grace. This behavior was unlike anything Sylvie had ever done, and she was truly worried now. She called her own office to take the rest of the day off, and left a message on her husband's voicemail to pick up the kids from school. She sped to Sylvie's house, her mind frantically making up horror stories about what she might find. She contemplated stopping at the store for chocolate, tequila, or a first-aid kit – supplies to cover any situation she might find when she arrived – but decided to go straight to the house to assess the situation first.

The door was unlocked and Colleen walked right in without knocking. In her haste, she slammed the door behind her and almost immediately heard the sound of shattering glass coming from the kitchen. She turned the corner, expecting the worst.

"Shit, Colleen, don't scare me like that. I broke my favorite mug." Sylvie reached for paper towels and began wiping up coffee and fragments of glass from the floor.

"Where the fuck have you been? I've called you repeatedly this week, and I've been worried sick! Grace is, too! I was beginning to think he killed you or kidnapped you!" She took a closer look at the scene, now that she had unburdened the worries on her mind, and felt a bit of relief that her friend seemed unharmed.

Sylvie's kitchen table was littered with papers and pens, partially full glasses with the dregs of different colored beverages, a plate with the crumbs of a breakfast, and a computer. Dishes were piled, unwashed, in her sink. It didn't appear that Sylvie had showered in a couple days– she was wearing black yoga pants and a large, loose t-shirt, with her uncombed hair piled up and pinned on top of her head. She looked happy, mopping up her floor with a smile on her face. Colleen was confused.

"I sent you a message, but then I turned off my phone. I took some time off work."

"I didn't get a message." Colleen looked around and spotted Sylvie's phone on the counter. She switched it on and waited, impatiently staring at the screen for it to spring to life. Sylvie took the phone from her and scrolled to her texts.

"Oh, I guess I forgot to press *send*. But look, I tried, it's still here." She handed the phone back to Colleen.

Hey! The date was amazing! Taking the week off to write. Talk soon.

"Sorry, guess I was too excited to check if it reached you. Didn't mean to make you worry."

Colleen grabbed Sylvie in a bear hug, and didn't let her go for several long moments. "You're okay, and that's great. Now would you please tell me what the fuck is going on?"

Sylvie disentangled herself from Colleen's arms and reached for a small stack of papers on the table. She led

Colleen to the couch in the living room, sat her down and put the papers in her hands.

"Read," she said.

I heard the doorbell ring, and my heart was pounding with anticipation. After months with almost no social activity, hoping I was using the time wisely to mend a broken heart after another bad relationship, I had finally agreed to be set up on a blind date. I wasn't sure if my heart was ready for it, or if my date would easily be able to see the bits of emotional tape still holding the pieces together. But I had consented to give it a try – I was beginning to feel lonely in my world populated only by couples, and wanted to start again. I yearned to have someone hold my hand and look at me with eyes that saw into my soul. I sent a silent prayer to the universe as I walked to the door, *please let this be okay*, and turned the handle.

Oh, what a sight he was to see, standing in my doorway. A bouquet of hand-picked tropical flowers was the first thing I noticed – red ginger, orange and blue bird of paradise, red and yellow heliconia, with sprays of fern and green ti leaves. A large, strong hand held them towards me. My eyes followed his hand along the curve of his arm, browned from the sun with tribal tattoos ending just below his elbow, and leading to the short sleeves of a cobalt blue, collared shirt with the top two buttons undone. A few wisps of hair from his tan chest reached out the top. My gaze finally lifted, and although I had seen him before, I had never stared directly at his face. He was beautiful and rugged – soft, slightly curly brown hair hung to both sides of his almond-shaped green eyes; his nose was long and thin, with the slightest hint of crookedness, as if he had been in a long-forgotten fight in his youth. His lips were full and red and turned up in a smile, under which was a strong chin, with the smallest depression of a dimple in the center. None of his features were perfect, but together they created a pleasing countenance – one I thought I could stare at for hours without tiring.

I skipped the formal introductions; there didn't seem to be a need for them. "Beautiful flowers," I said. "Did you pick them yourself?"

"They're mostly from my yard, with a couple from my neighbor's."

"Do you always steal your neighbor's flowers for your dates?" I teased as I reached out to take the bouquet.

"She lets me pick what I like. I carry her heavy groceries into her house; lately, I think she only goes shopping when she knows I'll be home to help," he said with an amused grin.

"I've barely met you and I'm already a little jealous of your neighbor."

"I'd like to tell her that. She's probably 70 years old, and I'm sure it's been a while since another woman was jealous of her." His amused grin widened to flash perfectly straight, white teeth.

I turned back into my doorway with the flowers, intending to put them in water before we left. "Would you like to come in for a moment before we go?"

"Just for a moment; we have reservations so we should leave soon." Michael followed me to my kitchen. He didn't sit, but leaned against the entry while I opened cabinets, wondering where I had last seen a vase.

Finally locating one large enough for the tropicals, I placed them inside and ran enough water into the vase to keep the heavy flowers from tipping it over. I set them in the center of my embarrassingly cluttered kitchen table and turned to look at Michael. He was casually leaning on his shoulder with his arms crossed in front of him, right leg slightly crossed over the left. I had felt that he had been watching me bustle about my kitchen instead of looking at his surroundings, but it didn't make me feel the least bit uncomfortable.

"Thank you for the flowers, they're perfect. Shall we go, or would you like a drink first?"

"Let's get to the restaurant. You live a bit out of the way, so we have some driving to do." He reached out for my hand.

I took his hand in my left and grabbed my purse off the table with my right, and let him lead me back toward the front door.

We walked together down the flower-bordered walkway to the street, where he had parked his blue Tacoma. "You must enjoy gardening yourself," he said, noticing the annuals planted along the pavement.

"I do, when I have time for it. Usually once a year I go into a plant frenzy and buy everything that looks pretty. It takes me weeks to finally get everything into the ground, and then I basically ignore them until they look bad. I like to think I'm helping local nurseries by killing my flowers regularly."

Michael graciously did not comment on my inability to keep flowers alive.

He opened the passenger door of his truck and helped me into the seat, then walked around the front to the driver's side. With a quick glance, I could tell he took pride in his truck, even though it was obviously used for construction work; it was immaculately clean despite the random power tools strewn throughout the back seat. A diamond-plate tool box took up a quarter of the back bed space, and lengths of wood were strapped to the racks.

"Where are we headed?" I asked as he turned the key in the ignition. "Or is it supposed to be a surprise?"

"East side. We're going to Duke's. They've got a pretty balanced menu, so even if you're a picky, vegan, gluten-intolerant eater we can still enjoy a meal together." His broad grin was obviously given to soften the barb, in case I actually was that kind of person – which I wasn't. I loved food of all types, and I told him so.

"Thank God. They serve great steaks, and I'd hate to feel guilty eating one if it offended you. Which I'd still do. But I'd feel bad about it. Kinda." I loved his smile.

We drove down the hill in silence; I didn't want to disturb his concentration on the sudden twists and turns of the narrow road to get to the highway. I was also taking the time to calm my rapidly-beating heart. I had been nervous about meeting Michael for the first time after so many months since I'd been on a successful date, but his carefree manner left me at ease. I was amazed to discover how calm I really was, and that my heart was pounding less than I expected, when I analyzed myself.

"You do construction for a living?" I wasn't sure if it sounded like a statement or a question after it came out of my mouth. I never considered myself a confident conversationalist, but work seemed like a good place to begin. Having several hours to talk to someone I had just met frightened me, just a little.

"Yes, according to my tax returns. I do finish carpentry for several builders on the island. After they complete the main structure, whether it's a house or restaurant or hotel, I go in and put on the little touches like window sills and bannisters and baseboards. I used to make custom cabinets, but most people aren't willing anymore to spend that much money for something they can order from *Home Depot*; sometimes I put different finishes on what they order, or change the hardware to something more elegant."

"According to your tax returns?" I asked. "Are you secretly a drug dealer?" I hoped that sounded like the joke it was meant to be.

Michael smiled. "No, I don't have enough patience to deal with the idiots who buy drugs. Well, that's not true, I do business with plenty of people who do all kinds of drugs, but I'm just not the one they depend on for what they consider happiness. I'm secretly a painter. I'm a typical starving artist with a day job. If I could spend my days painting portraits or landscapes I would. But lately I've been making custom frames for my friends' artwork, and I've been trying to figure out how to make that a full-time job."

I was surprised. Michael wasn't the stereotypical hot, dumb construction worker everyone imagined he was, including myself. He was an artist at heart, doing what he had to to pay his bills.

"How did you get into making frames? And how do you decide what kind of frame would look appropriate for someone's art?" I silently applauded myself for coming up with an intelligent-sounding question to keep him talking.

He paused for a moment before answering, a thoughtful look on his face. I hadn't stopped staring at his profile since we started driving, and I wondered if that made him self-conscious, but I couldn't help it – he was so easy to look at.

He took his eyes off the road to glance at me, as if reading my mind. The carefree smile was still there.

"My mother was a painter. She was also a high school art teacher. My father was a carpenter. They both taught me what they knew. My father didn't like to be bored, so when he retired he started making frames for the dozens of paintings my mom had stashed around the house. He was a great wood-worker, but not what you'd call an artist, mostly functional carpentry. He'd surprise my mom with a new frame on a painting, something he'd spend days making in secret in his workshop; sometimes she'd like it, but more often she didn't. I'd be over for dinner and have to listen to hours of arguments about why the choice of wood didn't match the painting's intent, or why the bevel wasn't complementary, stuff like that. It's incredible what you can learn just by listening to people argue."

"Do your parents still live nearby?" I asked.

"No, they both died a few years back. But they had a great marriage, and were happy together, despite their artistic differences – I hope I didn't make it sound as if all they did was argue. I'm an only child, so I moved back home after my father died, and my mom followed him shortly after. They had their own work spaces for carpentry and painting, and I use them both now."

I sat in silence for a mile or two; he had given me a lot of information to digest in a short space of time. I wasn't sure if I should express my condolences for the loss of his parents, or just continue on in the conversation. Michael saved me from making the choice, again as if reading my mind.

"So you asked how I decide what kind of frame to make for someone else's art. To make a long story short, I rarely make that decision. My house is like a gallery for frames in every type of wood, of all different designs. Towards the end, my dad started experimenting with scroll work on the frames, carving these intricate patterns in the wood. I think he started experimenting with that because he found a cheap saw he didn't own and wanted to see what he could do with it. Drove my mom crazy. They'd finally agree on a particular frame for a particular painting, then she'd come home and there'd be vines of leaves, or hearts, cut into it, just because he wanted to see what it would look like. So people come by my house with their own ideas, good or bad, or pick something they like from what my father created. I've learned not to try to talk people out of their ideas, even if I don't like them. I've sat through enough of those arguments. I just make what they tell me to make."

Michael turned the truck and pulled into the restaurant parking lot. This trip to the east side seemed shorter than the normal trip by myself – I felt a tinge of worry that time would go by too fast on our date. It had just started but I already wished it would last forever.

We found a parking spot in the busy lot as another car was leaving, and Michael said "Wait here," as he climbed out of the truck. He walked around to my side and opened the door, holding out his hand as if I needed help. I didn't, but I took his hand anyway. That small, unexpected gesture, along with the touch of his rough hand, made my heart melt. He walked me across a wooden bridge over a stream, which led to a paved path to Duke's.

At the last moment before Michael showed up at my house I had made the decision to wear soft, comfortable sandals instead of the spikey high heels that looked ultra-sexy on my long legs. I was glad of that decision as I walked over the wooden bridge, which was full of pits and cracks from age. I wasn't worried about tripping and falling in front of my date with my low-heeled shoes, and they put me an inch shorter than him when we stood next to each other. As a tall woman, I like a man who is taller than me, and if I have to sacrifice clumsiness for height then I made the right decision. I clung to his arm as we approached the hostess stand at the restaurant's entrance – I didn't need to hold onto him for balance, but it felt so right. Michael gave his name and we were led to a perfectly quiet table for two, overlooking a koi pond on the floor below. The hostess left menus, and directly behind her was a waitress with glasses of water and a list of the night's specials. She told us about the seared ahi, caught just that morning, and the opah with mango-avocado salsa, then asked for our drink order.

Michael looked at me, expecting me to order first.

"A glass of your house cabernet, please," I told the waitress.

She turned to Michael for his order, her smile just a shade brighter for such a good-looking man. I couldn't blame her – he was *that* good looking.

"I'd like a rum and Coke," he said. "Dark rum."

"I'll get your drinks and be back for your order," the waitress said, leaving us alone.

I studied the menu, but knew I'd probably order one of the fish specials at the last minute. I looked over the top of my menu at Michael, who was sitting back in his chair sipping his water.

"I can never decide what I want when I eat here," I told him. "Everything is always so good. But I really like how they prepare the fresh fish." I sincerely wished I was more skilled at making interesting conversation.

"Do you come here very often?"

"No," I replied. "If I eat out it's usually with friends who have small children, so they pick a place where it's more acceptable to make a mess. Usually somewhere outdoors where the birds fly around and eat the bits of food the kids drop under the table. Easier on the waitress, plus the birds help keep the kids entertained."

"So you only come here on dates? I feel pretty unoriginal now," Michael joked.

"I *have* been here on a date or two, but that's not enough to make it unoriginal, considering I've lived here for 15 years. Mostly I've come here with my parents when they visit. But they haven't been able to visit for a couple years, so it's probably been that long since I've come here."

"Does that mean you haven't been on a date in a couple years, or do you just take them somewhere else now?" I was wondering when someone would bring up dating history, and was glad Michael mentioned it first. He was so self-confident that his question didn't seem possessive or jealous, as I imagined it might if I had asked that same question. This man had confidence and ease emanating from him, enough to bolster my own flagging belief in myself.

"My dating life has not been spectacular in recent years, so yes, I've been on dates, no, they haven't been at this particular restaurant, and another no, they typically aren't worth a second try." I breathed in some of his oozing confidence. "It's been a while since I've had a boyfriend," I volunteered.

Michael opened his mouth to reply, and at that exact moment, the waitress reappeared at our table with the drinks. I'd never been so disappointed to get a drink in my life.

"Wine," she said, placing a glass to my left. "And rum and Coke. Have you decided on your order?"

Again, Michael stared at me, expecting me to place my order first.

"I'll try the opah special," I answered.

"I'd like the New York steak, medium rare," Michael said as he took my menu and handed them both to the waitress. "And can we start with an order of calamari?" He looked at me, "You like calamari?"

"Yes, perfect."

The waitress repeated our order back to us, waited for our assent, and left us alone again. I took a sip of my wine, unsure of how to get back into our previous topic of conversation. Again, Michael came to my rescue, and again, I was amazed at how easily conversation came to him.

"You don't look like someone who hasn't had a boyfriend in a long time. Honestly, when the ladies at the bank were describing you, and I knew exactly who they were talking about, I had a hard time believing you were single. I've seen you several times but I don't think you ever noticed me. You always looked so preoccupied so I never spoke to you – but I wanted to."

My heart fluttered. "I *was* preoccupied. Staring at you when you weren't looking." I didn't mention his ass, which was mainly what I had been preoccupied with.

Michael blushed, staring at the table. Then he looked directly into my eyes, smiling. "Well, I'm glad we got that out of the way." I took a sip of my wine to hide my own blushing face.

"I never imagined you were single, either," I told him. "If Crystal hadn't convinced me to leave my business card for you we wouldn't be here. I guess we owe her for setting us up." I paused. "Unless you have some crazy ex-girlfriends I'll need to watch out for?"

"I do have some ex-girlfriends, and none were happy when we broke up, but I don't think envy will make anyone go off the deep end. You're safe."

I laughed. "Good. My fighting skills aren't what they used to be."

"You'd fight for me?" he smiled slyly at me as he asked.

"We'll see how the rest of our date goes before I promise anything."

The waitress cheerfully appeared with our calamari.

"Enjoy. Your dinner will be out shortly." We both picked up our forks and added calamari to our appetizer plates.

"Make sure you get plenty of the sauce – it's so good," Michael told me, spooning a generous portion of the creamy red-orange liquid onto my plate.

We enjoyed the calamari in a few moments of silence.

"Good choice," I said after a few bites. "Does this mean that *you* bring dates here so often that you know the menu?" I looked up at him with my own sly grin.

Michael slowly sipped his rum and Coke before answering, staring straight into my eyes while he thought. "I'm trying to decide if I should lie to make you jealous."

"I'm already jealous of all the other women you've dated; you don't need to make it worse," I joked as I helped myself to more of the appetizer.

"I've brought a few women here, sure, but there's something about the way they prepare their steaks. I eat here nearly every time I have a job on this side of town; by myself or sometimes I can convince one of the guys to come with me after work. Nothing like a good steak after a long day."

"I guess physical labor is like that – I crave more meat after working out. I sit at a desk most days and tend to eat salads for dinner."

"You're an accountant?" Michael asked. "That's what the ladies at the bank told me."

"Yes, according to my tax returns." I had been waiting to use his same line, and he recognized it.

"So you're secretly a drug dealer, too."

I laughed, and took another sip of wine to let him wonder. Before I could answer, the waitress approached with two plates balanced on a tray. She placed our meals in front of us, and took our used appetizer dishes.

"Be careful, the plates are hot. Can I get either of you another drink?"

"Another glass of wine would be great," I said.

Michael put his hand over his glass. "I'm driving. Just more water, please."

The waitress left and we started in on our entrées. My fish was white and flaky, cooked expertly, and the mango-avocado salsa blended perfectly with the flavor. I asked how his steak was done. It took a few moments before he could answer; he had a dreamy look on his face.

"You *have* to try this," he answered, cutting a piece and holding it out to me. "It's unbelievable."

I took the bite from his fork with a comfort level beyond what I normally find on a first date. Everything felt so natural with Michael.

We spent the next few minutes with full mouths, enjoying our dinner. I was finishing my grilled vegetables when Michael spoke again.

"So, you're a drug dealer with a respectable side job," he made a sound that was something between a giggle and a laugh. It was a very masculine sound, though. "That's a good cover. If I was a cop and pulled you over I'd never guess you had a trunk full of cocaine. You look extremely innocent."

"Maybe I should get into that line of business, then. I never gave much thought to how little I resemble a gangster. Probably good money to be made," I replied with a thoughtful look on my face, as if I was considering the idea.

"Are you going to make me guess, then? Okay. Exotic dancer. But you had to take an accounting job because there aren't any strip clubs nearby."

"Ha!" I laughed, almost spraying him with the sip of wine I had just taken. "I can barely walk without tripping when I'm barefoot, much less dance on a stage wearing those crazy, platform stripper heels. Men would only put money in my g-string because they felt sorry for me, trying to support my four kids."

"Do you have kids? I never thought to ask," he said, looking a little surprised.

"Yes, four of them. From four different fathers. I just told you that." I tried to look serious, but failed.

Our waitress came by again to clear our plates and asked if we wanted dessert or coffee. Michael looked me in the eye and earnestly said, "You'll get more dollar bills in your g-string if you have a little more meat on your bones. Guys like a stripper with some curves. Get the hula pie."

The waitress opened her mouth in shock, looking at me, but nothing came out. This time I couldn't suppress a laugh, and I had to quickly sit forward and press my napkin to my chin to prevent wine from dribbling onto my dress. Michael looked on with a mischievous sparkle in his eyes.

"I think we'll just take the check, please," he told the waitress, never taking his eyes off me.

"You're not a drug dealer, you're not a stripper, and you're obviously not the straight-man in a comedy routine. I'll figure out your heart's secret desire before the end of our evening."

I smiled at him, my composure not entirely back. I hadn't intended on keeping my passion for writing a secret, but I loved how flirty our conversation had become and didn't want it to end.

"Okay, let's make a bet," I said. "If you can guess what I'd rather be doing for a living you'll win a prize."

"What's the prize? I need to decide if it's worth working for."

"If you win, I'll kiss you goodnight." I was holding my breath, somehow worried he wouldn't think that was a worthwhile payment.

"All that effort for a kiss? Are you talking about a quick little peck on the cheek, or a long, slow one? I have to know how hard I need to try."

"A long one if you win. A tiny peck on the cheek if you lose."

"So I'm guaranteed some sort of kiss at the end of our evening, regardless of whether I win or lose? I can live with that."

"But who's to say if we end up on a second date? Wouldn't you rather try for the big prize, in case we never see each other again?"

"I'm not worried about that," Michael said confidently. "We'll be going out again, and it's only a matter of time before I get the real kiss." As I gazed into his bright green eyes, I knew this was true, and wondered how I would be able to keep from really kissing him tonight, or immediately for that matter, if he didn't guess correctly.

The waitress arrived with our bill, but before I had a chance to reach into my purse Michael gave her his credit card, and she walked away.

"With four kids to raise, and probably no child support from the four deadbeat dads, at least let me buy you dinner." He would have made a good straight-man.

I couldn't stop thinking about the promised kiss at the end of the night and the stubborn smile would not leave my face. I wondered how it was possible that the evening was going so smoothly, in light of my past dating disasters, and realized that my heart had kicked its tempo up a notch. I wondered if he could tell. He still looked as calm as ever, leaning back in his chair and watching me, with an amused look on his face.

The waitress returned Michael's credit card, he signed the check and stood up. "Shall we? It's a beautiful night, why don't we go for a walk on the beach?"

The moon was almost full, and cast a trail of sparkling light on the water that lit our way along the path. Michael took my hand as we walked.

"Do I need to get you home so you can put all your kids to bed?"

"No, they're used to being home all night by themselves while I work. They'll get tired of fighting over crackers and TV channels and fall asleep eventually."

He stopped walking and turned me to face him. "Seriously, though, do you have kids? It wouldn't be a bad thing, but I'm curious."

"No, no kids. What about you? Am I going to find out that you're only stuck being a carpenter because you have a string of baby mamas to support?"

He laughed, and we continued walking. The path was surprisingly empty for a Saturday night. "I'm in the same situation as you. No kids, not even by accident. I'm a carpenter because I haven't worked up the courage to rely on what I love for my living. I've never even taken my work to the local galleries."

"But you seem so confident about everything; I find it hard to believe you don't have your paintings displayed everywhere. I imagine you could sell a used car to a blind man on charm alone."

"Well that's part of the problem," he said. "I don't want to sell them because I'm charming, I want to sell them because they're good." He pulled my hand and spun me into his arms, the moonlight showing me a very serious look on his face. "I'm fully aware of how charming I am." His serious face changed to a devilish smile, impossible to resist, especially now that his arms were around me.

"I'm a writer," I blurted out, wanting desperately for him to claim the grand prize of the evening. I was hopelessly attracted to him, and combined with the romantic scenery and his warm embrace, this was the storybook moment for our first kiss.

He immediately let go of me, but took my hand again and continued our walk. I tried not to let the disappointment show on my face.

"I was going to make my next guess, but now you've gone and given away the answer. I'm not sure if that means you forfeit and I win, or if the bet is off and we both lose. I had some great occupations lined up for you."

"Like what?" I asked.

He ignored my question. "Do I read your articles in the paper and not know it, or are there stacks of books you've written in the library?"

"Neither," I answered. "I've written one book and I'm fairly certain you wouldn't have read it."

"I enjoy the occasional book, how do you know I haven't read it?"

"I'm pretty sure only my friends bought it, that's why I'm still an accountant."

"What's it about?"

"It's a travel book."

"Are you working on anything right now?"

I hesitated before answering. I was working on a romance novel, but the project was known only to my best friend. I wasn't ready to share this information with him yet, for fear he would think I had only gone out with him to get notes for my book – which was partly true in the beginning.

"I'm trying to write fiction this time. I've wanted to be a writer since I can remember, but I was always afraid to try. My first book was a good start, and it helped me realize I could actually write a book. This next one will be the test to see if I can create something wholly from my imagination."

"What's it about?" Michael asked.

"I could tell you, but then I'd have to kill you," I joked, hoping to lighten the mood and change the subject.

"Secret agent – that was going to be my next guess before you gave it away," he said, referring back to our bet on my hidden ambition.

"Accounting would be a great cover for a secret agent," I said sarcastically. "My reading glasses are actually x-ray specs, and the different pens in my pocket-protector squirt acid and have radio transmitters."

"Do you have a secret, stylish sports car that you use when you're on assignment?" he asked.

"I use the Ranger – it helps me with my cover. But it has a Ferrari engine in it."

The thought of a high-speed chase in my 12-year-old, slightly rusty, brown truck made us both laugh. We continued our walk, hand in hand, until we reached Michael's own truck in the parking lot.

"I'd better get you home before your imaginary kids kill each other," he said as he opened my door and helped me into my seat.

He looked at me, the moonlight shining in his beautiful green eyes. "Right now, I'm glad you don't live with your four kids." He closed my door and walked to his side, getting in. "I'd hate to cause a disturbance when I claim my grand prize on your doorstep."

"I'm not sure you qualify for the grand prize," I replied, feeling flirty again. "You didn't actually win."

"The only reason I didn't win is because you forfeited. I would have come up with the answer, eventually. I saw your computer, a notebook and a bunch of nice pens on your table. I don't think accountants record transactions in hand-written ledgers anymore." I hadn't given him enough credit for checking out his surroundings during the brief time he had spent in my kitchen; he had surprised me several times during the evening, and it made me long to give him his prize even more.

Already nervous about what kind of kiss would transpire when we reached my house, I had a hard time getting control of my fluttering heart. As Michael backed out of the parking spot and navigated his way to the exit, I used the time to remind myself that I deserved to be treated like a goddess, and I deserved to have a beautiful man kiss me passionately, but only if he deserved it, too. Gone were the days that I would kiss someone, just to be kissed. He had to earn it, and so far, he had done a spectacular job of doing so. Only the ride home was left to decide the final outcome, and being present, rather than concentrating on my anxiety over the future, was the only way to proceed. I willed my heart to relax, because eventually it would get what it wanted.

"What do you do when you're not working or painting?" I asked him.

"Besides taking beautiful women on dates?" he laughed. "That takes up *a lot* of my time."

"I imagine it does. A charming guy like you has to have a pretty full dance card. But suppose you had a free day to do anything you wanted, by yourself or with one of your many admirers, how would you spend it?"

He looked thoughtful in the greenish glow from the dashboard lights. "I would probably be out looking for new inspirations for my painting, assuming that my laundry was done and I had food in my refrigerator."

"Necessary, sure, housekeeping is important. But I don't want to be your typical date," I said sarcastically. "Where do you like to go to find inspiration?"

"I like to paint people and landscapes, even better if it's both together. Sometimes I drag my gear on a hike if it's a nice day, and sit and paint whatever catches my eye. Sometimes I take my camera, then go home to paint one of the pictures I took, surfers or sunrises maybe. Lately I've been swimming more, I thought I'd try some underwater landscapes. But I'm not a great swimmer, and if I actually swim out far enough to see something interesting that I'd like to capture in a painting, I'm so preoccupied with staying above water that I forget the details."

"You should try using water wings; they work for my friends' kids."

"Great suggestion, thanks. But I'm not sure they make them in my size." My eyes were drawn to his biceps; not the bulging, veiny type from weight lifting, but chiseled from a life of labor and regular exercise.

"I swim all the time. And I have an underwater camera. Maybe I can interest you in going for a swim with me tomorrow, if you're not too busy with your many time-consuming household chores." I was sure he'd look as good in swim trunks as he did fully clothed, but the sooner I got to see for myself, the better.

"You're asking me on a date tomorrow?" he asked. "Swimming?"

"If you'd rather take me to Safeway, I'd understand. But yes, would you like to go on a swimming date with me?"

"I would love to. I've never been on a swimming date before. And you'll bring your camera?"

"I'll charge the battery the moment I get home," I answered.

"Not the exact moment you get home, I think we have some unfinished business about our bet," Michael reminded me.

"True, but whether you won or lost, or if I forfeited by giving away the answer, I reserve the right to decide on your prize. It could be a matter of a second, with a simple peck on your cheek, before I send you on your way."

He laughed. "What's the point of making a bet if you're just going to arbitrarily decide on the outcome? You don't play fair."

"All is fair in love and war," I quoted to him. "Surely you've realized this with your vast dating experience?"

Michael didn't answer, but continued to drive, with a smile lighting up his face. We reached the turnoff for my street, and proceeded up the dark, winding road to my house. This time, when we arrived, he pulled his truck into my driveway and parked behind my Ranger. Michael hopped out and quickly ran to my side as I was opening my door. He extended his hand to help me down, and walked me up the path to my house. Once there, he turned to face me before I could unlock the front door. I was fumbling for the keys in the bottom of my purse; anxiety was creeping back into my body and I needed some activity to hide it. I finally located the keys and, with slightly trembling fingers, slipped the correct key into the lock, but didn't turn it.

"Win or lose, I guess my fate is in your hands," he whispered as he took me in his arms. "Which will it be?"

I left the keys hanging in the lock and wrapped my arms around his shoulders, pulling him close to my body. He was warm and strong, and I wanted him to win – the grand prize, and so much more.

"Technically, I did ruin the bet," I started, not wanting to end the flirty tone of our evening, while moving my face to a fraction of an inch away from his. "You're justified in expecting a long kiss. But do you think you deserve one?"

"I think I do," he answered simply.

I agreed, and lifted myself on my toes to close the final distance between us. His lips felt soft against mine, and he kissed me with a passion that made me forget that anything else existed around us. The world spun, keeping time as usual, but I ceased to notice – it could have been minutes or days while we stood there in each other's arms, and I never wanted it to end.

Colleen looked up at Sylvie as she finished reading the final page.

"Isn't this supposed to be a romance novel? Where's the sex?" she asked.

"Don't you think it was romantic?"

"You took a week out of your life to write this, and scared everyone half-to-death, and you didn't even get laid?" Colleen was indignant.

Sylvie smiled at her. "You'll just have to wait for the next chapter," she replied, and walked to the kitchen to pour them both a glass of tequila.

Many thanks to Soren Velice for his editing talents. A former print journalist, Soren has edited both of my books, and hopefully many more to come. He has helped me become a better writer through the liberal and judicious use of his red pen.

Cover artwork and graphic design by Jessica Quetula
    Author photo by Shanti Manzano

Thank you to my test readers for their comments, corrections and encouragement – Donna Burovac, Colleen Kaiminaauao, Dana Miyake and Cynthia Dazzi.

Melissa Burovac is a writer and photographer living on Kauai. An avid outdoorswoman, she enjoys paddling – one-man, six-man and SUP – surfing, scuba diving, swimming, yoga and running. She is always ready for adventure and loves doing things that scare her a little.

Melissa's first book *Wandering* tells the hilarious tale of her solo travels from Mexico through Central America, Cuba, Australia, Cambodia and Thailand. As someone with no sense of direction, no ability to plan, and plenty of social anxiety, her experiences prove that anyone who wants to travel *can*! Sometimes you just need to pack a bag and get lost.